A Forbidden Love

SCOTTISH WEREBEARS BOOK 3

LORELEI MOONE

CONTENTS

PROLOGUE

It had started like any other day. The boy couldn't wait to get out of the house and head to the beach at Applecross Bay. It was his favorite place in the world and nothing or no one could keep him away.

"Don't go in the water, all right? You'll catch a cold. And keep an eye on your brother." The boy's mother called after him from the veranda but he barely reacted, just kept his eyes fixed on the horizon. "Did you hear me?"

"Yes, mom." He took his little brother by the hand and dragged him along the narrow pathway through the dunes, around the s-bend uphill until their mother was out of view and they reached the crest of the hillock that stood between them and the windswept beach. He was twelve years old, old enough to know not to go into the icy waters. Old enough to take his brother to the beach. Not that his mother had realized that fact – she still acted like he was a baby.

It was chilly and cloudy, a typical Scottish summer's day, but the boys were used to it. Applecross Bay was where they were born, where they belonged.

"Shall we finish that sand castle?" asked the smaller of the two, who couldn't have been older than seven or eight years old, looking up at his older brother with big blue eyes.

"Don't be stupid, the tide will have washed everything away overnight," the older boy responded.

"So we start again. Make a better one?"

The older boy shrugged. "You do it."

"Okay, I will."

They walked on further, downhill and finally across the damp sand until they almost reached the water. The beach was vast and pretty much empty, like most of the surrounding countryside. Some might say this place was desolate or lonely, but to anyone who knew better it was magical and full of endless possibilities.

The older boy let go of his kid brother's hand and watched as he ran the rest of the way, plastic bucket and spade in hand, ready to leave his mark on the landscape. Let him build another stupid sand castle. Let it get destroyed again when the high tide rolls in.

He had other ideas, as he tightened his grip around the net in his hand. He was going to climb the cliffs that marked the edge of the beach and catch some dinner. Sandcastles were for kids, but gathering food, that was a much more respectable and grown-up activity.

A quick look back at where his brother had started digging in the sand revealed that all was still as it should be. The beach was empty as always. Why was his mother so paranoid about them coming out here? It made no sense. Nothing ever happened here, and his little brother knew better than to get into the treacherous waters.

So he pushed onward against the strong winds coming in from the sea, straight towards the shiny black cliffs where he knew a lot of crabs and other wildlife liked to hide. He had seen a lobster there previously, and today was the day he would catch it. He was determined.

Anyone could pick up crabs from the beach; that required no skill. But lobsters were a lot more skittish and cunning.

The boy's determination grew as he clambered up the slippery rocks heading for the crevice where he'd seen his prey before. If only he could shift already, it would make things like climbing up rocks a lot easier. But he wasn't ready yet.

It was around the thirteenth year that the bear side would become strong enough to assert itself. How he wished he could just skip this last year and become fully bear already. But time neither waited nor sped up for anyone, unfortunately.

From the corner of his eye, the boy saw a movement. An animal? Perhaps a bird, trying to hunt for the same thing as him?

Looking back down at the beach, he saw his little brother was completely oblivious to anything around him. He just kept filling his little bucket and turning it over to make turret shaped piles of sand, haphazardly positioned next to each other. It was childish. Amateurish.

So the older boy once again focused on the task at hand. He wasn't about to give up that lobster to a seagull or something. No. That would be unacceptable.

But when he looked around again he saw that the earlier movement hadn't been a seagull or other animal. Further up the cliff, gazing down at him, sat a girl. Red hair blowing in the wind, framing a freckly face featuring two piercing green eyes. She was pretty, for a girl, and about his age.

"Hi," the redhead said.

The boy paused for a moment. Was he imagining this? Nobody ever came here, except a few of the locals. And he'd never seen her before. "Hi."

"Nice place. You live here?" she asked, while wrapping her arms around herself as though she was trying to keep warm.

"Uh-huh. Where are you from?"

"Edinburgh. We're only here on vacation."

"Aha. Edinburgh," the boy repeated after her, hoping it

made him sound knowledgeable. The truth was he'd never been to Edinburgh, or even spent much time away from his home just across the dunes at all.

"What's your name?" she asked.

"Jamie. Yours?" he responded.

But she didn't answer. Instead she got up on top of the cliff and looked back at something - he wasn't sure at what, because he was too far down to be able to catch her line of sight.

"Hey, I need to go. My dad gets real upset when he doesn't know where I am. See you around, maybe."

Before he had the chance to think of anything else to say, she had climbed over the other side of the cliffs, and ran off into the grass-covered dunes leading away from the beach. Perhaps he should follow her, try to get to know her. But he couldn't bring himself to move, so he just stood there watching as she got smaller and smaller and finally vanished over the top of the hill.

It was the strangest thing. When she was gone and out of sight, he wasn't even sure anymore if she'd actually been here or if he'd just imagined her. Nah, that was dumb. If he was going to imagine someone, he'd imagine someone totally different, not a *girl*. He didn't like girls much, thought they were mostly daft and spent way too much time fussing about stupid things like ponies and whatnot. No, he definitely wouldn't dream up a girl if it was up to him.

The entire incident had distracted him sufficiently that he didn't feel up to the task of hunting his arch nemesis, the lobster, anymore. So he climbed down the cliff from the end where he had just come from and walked across the beach towards the beginnings of his brother's sand castle.

The beach was empty again. Totally empty, like it

usually was. The bright red plastic bucket and spade were lying in the center of the oddly shaped circle of sand turrets. There was no sign of his brother.

Weird, had he gone back?

The boy traced their steps back to the path they had taken across the dunes. *He must have just gone home, right?* As he got further and further away from the water, his heart beat faster and a sense of panic built in his chest. Why would he just leave? He wouldn't. They'd only just gotten here and his castle was far from finished. There's no way his little brother would have left his bucket behind either.

He was completely out of breath by the time he made it home. His mom was sitting on the porch, reading her morning paper. As soon as she noticed him, she looked up and smiled.

"Hey, Jamie. That was quick. Where's Matty?" she asked.

He didn't know what to say to her exactly, how to explain it. At this moment Jamie realized two things: his brother was gone, and he'd never spend time down at the beach again.

CHAPTER ONE

It was late and most of Edinburgh's popular pubs were starting to close. Jamie Abbott didn't feel like heading home yet, but figured he might as well try to rest before another undoubtedly long day at the office.

A confusing maelstrom of thoughts plagued him. He had worked for the Alliance for years, laboring away day after day without much to show for it. Until now. Now they'd captured some actual members of the illustrious secret organization of humans who were trying to eliminate shifters the world over: the Sons of Domnall.

Three of them in total were being held in the basement underneath the Alliance office, while the rest had gotten away. Jamie thought about their unwillingness to talk. They may have made progress identifying and attacking what could very well be the base of the Sons of Domnall in Edinburgh, but what if they wouldn't learn much as a result? The only one who had said anything to him during questioning was the man in charge, who Jamie's colleague Aidan had identified as Lee Campbell.

Jamie knew better than to ask Aidan how he had uncovered the man's identity or what history they shared. If Jamie started digging into Aidan's private affairs, he could be certain to receive the same treatment in return. That was something Jamie was keen to avoid. Although Jamie was the senior Alliance member at the office, technically, when push came to shove that wouldn't mean very much to Aidan. Bears weren't good at dealing with authority figures like wolves were. They valued their autonomy too much, so team work didn't come naturally to them.

As Jamie had tried to gain further insights into the Sons and their activities in the city through intense interrogations, Campbell had been a constant source of frustration. He liked to speak in riddles. Jamie wasn't sure anything the man had told him was true. His gut told him that the one thing Campbell had definitely not lied about was that the Sons would plan a counterattack. They didn't take kindly to people, shifters in particular, interfering with their affairs and taking their members - brothers, as they called them - prisoner.

But Jamie and his people had always been careful. The building they occupied was owned by another, much more senior Alliance member, who had registered it in the name of a shell company. As far as the outside world was concerned, it was an administrative office for a shipping company.

After wandering the largely empty streets for about fifteen minutes, Jamie made it home. An impressive wooden door led to the ground floor of a Victorian house that had been converted into flats.

Jamie had been occupying this space for the better part of three years now. Despite splurging on the finest furniture to make it as comfortable as possible, he barely spent time here. Somehow, no matter what he did, he found it impossible to feel at home anywhere.

Jamie lived for his work, just like everyone else at the Alliance seemed to do. After hours, Jamie felt like he was waiting. For something, or someone. *The girl? How ridiculous.*

He took off his leather jacket and hung it neatly on one of the elegant dining chairs he never used. Then he checked his mail, even though he already knew that all he had waiting for him were bills.

It was four in the morning, according to the wall clock at the other end of the combined living and dining space. Jamie settled down in the armchair facing the TV that hung above the defunct period fireplace, but didn't switch it on.

How could he convince those people to talk? They were fanatics who truly believed in their cause and that made them dangerous.

Hell, we truly believe in ours too, don't we? Jamie sighed deeply and rubbed his temples in an attempt to soothe the dull ache that usually started to build up in there around this time. He knew he was exhausted, but he also knew sleep wouldn't find him just yet.

He closed his eyes and went through a few breathing exercises he'd found online. With his eyes still shut, he breathed in sharply, then exhaled in a slow, controlled manner for as long as he could stretch it. Rinse and repeat.

It wouldn't work, he already knew that, but he was nothing if not persistent in everything he did.

After a few breaths like that, he opened his eyes again and started to look at the switched off TV. Jamie felt his body relax, the tension he'd been carrying around in his limbs slowly dissipating until his body was ready for sleep. The previously clear shape of the television blurred in front of him as he continued to stare at it.

His mind refused to cooperate with his body's demand for rest, though.

He needed to get those men to talk.

Perhaps they knew something that would help him.

Jamie's eyelids grew heavy until he gave in and let them fall shut again. He was surrounded by darkness, but only for a moment, before the blackest of black made way for the gray late summer's day that always came to him at this time of night. That day at the beach, back when he was only twelve years old. The day his brother had gone missing.

The pain of the loss stabbed him right through the heart, as it had done back then, when he first realized what had happened. But that wasn't the worst of it. The worst thing was that his baby brother was only a small part of what plagued his mind.

The girl.

He couldn't get the girl out of his head.

It made no sense at all. Why was he so fixated on her? He didn't remember when exactly the memories had started to change, because it had been so gradual at first. As the years had passed, so had his recollection of that day. Every night when these glimpses of so long ago infiltrated his mind against his will, the girl had aged right along with Jamie.

They'd been probably the same age back then. Tonight what Jamie saw wasn't an awkward twelve year old, but a full-figured redhead in her thirties, like him. And so lifelike, too. Her green eyes sparkled in what little light could escape the hazy clouds overhead. Her smile could stop traffic, it was so radiant. Her ample curves invited further scrutiny, but Jamie resisted the temptation, as usual.

Sometimes he did allow himself to focus on her beauty, just for a bit. But the guilt always got him in the end. It wasn't worth it. How could he fantasize about some girl he might have very well just imagined there on the beach, when his actual, real little brother had vanished without a trace?

How could a creature so beautiful have existed in the exact same moment as a loss so terrible?

His inner bear kept insisting that if only he found her,

everything would become whole again. Secretly that was why he'd joined the Alliance in Edinburgh rather than anywhere else, because that's where she'd said she lived. If he found her, perhaps he'd find *him* too. But if he found *her*, did it matter?

Jamie frowned, furious at himself for even questioning the importance of figuring out what had happened to his brother. Angry for all the pain the disappearance had caused to his parents, who had never been the same since. Guilty over his own selfishness and carelessness. It had all been his fault, after all.

Breathe in deeply, hold, slowly release. *Who was she, though?*

Breathe in, and release. *Why was she so important?*

Breathe and release.

————— ◆ —————

When Jamie awoke, he had no idea just when he'd fallen asleep, or for how long. He wasn't rested, but it was enough. He got up and stretched himself. Sleeping in a chair wasn't ideal, but it was better than not sleeping at all. A big mug of sweet instant coffee later, he felt ready for the day that lay ahead.

He would question the prisoners some more today. And today was the day Aidan would bring in their human informant, Alison, for more thorough questioning as well. Perhaps she knew more than she'd initially shared. Jamie was also curious about how she knew about the websites in the first place. She'd been too vague about that in the past. Either way, it was time for Jamie to step in and take control of the situation before the Sons got the chance to plan anything.

The first order of business would be to set up an

appropriate area for them to question Alison. There was no way he would let her into the main office, and he certainly couldn't use the basement where the prisoners were kept. Perhaps one of the rooms upstairs...

Jamie could be the most single-minded and focused person in the morning, but come nightfall, his thoughts went everywhere at once. Somehow it was easier to keep the bear part of him under control when the sun was out. It was his bear who was suffering more than his human side.

Now that it was morning, the world made sense again. Jamie grabbed his things and made the trip to the office on foot like he often did when the weather allowed it. A bit of drizzle like today wasn't enough of a deterrent.

"Morning." Jamie greeted the rest of the team as he swung the door open. Aidan and Heidi were already sitting at their work stations, while their resident computer genius, Kyle, was pouring himself a cup of coffee in the corner.

"Anything I need to know before getting things ready for Alison later?" Jamie asked.

Aidan looked up from his desk, as did Heidi. In the couple of days since her rescue, both of their behavior had changed drastically. They'd been distant toward each other earlier, especially Heidi, but now they seemed to have connected in a way one doesn't often see. Like they understood what the other was thinking without voicing it.

Jamie knew what it meant - they were mates, despite belonging to different species - and he'd tried to talk to them about it, but they were intent on keeping a low profile. Jamie couldn't blame them. Wolves and bears didn't ordinarily get along and there would be many who would oppose the idea of interspecies mating.

He suppressed a smile as he watched them exchange a

subtle glance. They were talking to each other, communicating with their thoughts alone. Rather than worry about their connection distracting from their work here, Jamie was certain it made them more valuable to their cause. He would never have to second guess their loyalties, as long as they were on the team together.

"No progress on the prisoners. We've been keeping the lights on in their cells to confuse their sense of time in the hopes that it would help us break them," Aidan said.

"I see. Perhaps the girl can give us something that'll help."

Aidan shrugged. Jamie could tell from his demeanor that he didn't think bringing the informant in would make any difference. But it was Jamie's responsibility as team leader to steer this investigation forward. If he was called in by the Alliance Council, he wanted to be able to say that he hadn't left any stone unturned. They'd given him this chance to make a difference at a time when he was completely lost. He owed it to them, as well as himself to do the best job he could.

"Very well, I'll get things ready for the interrogation," Jamie said. "Kyle, walk with me?"

Jamie pushed the door leading to the staircase open and waited while Kyle caught up, steaming cup of coffee in hand. "I'm thinking of converting one of the upstairs rooms so we can use it for interrogations. The one closest to the back entrance. I want you to think about recording solutions."

Kyle followed him up the stairs as the door slowly shut behind them with an ominous creak.

"Right. I'm assuming you don't want to make things too obvious?" Kyle asked.

"Hidden cameras. Multiple angles."

"Sure thing. I have some equipment lying around that

would be perfect. It'll take me a couple of hours maximum to set everything up." Kyle said.

"Wonderful. Let me know if you need any help." Jamie smiled. They'd all struggled to get along initially, but the team was finally pulling together as one. If they wanted to be successful in their fight against the Sons of Domnall, they needed to keep this up.

CHAPTER TWO

"This is a bloody disaster," Alison Campbell whispered, while sinking back into the sofa and shaking her head.

"Yep," her brother Gareth, who was sitting opposite her, confirmed.

"How did the Alliance find them, you think?" Alison asked.

"No idea, perhaps someone talked. Or perhaps they managed to sniff us out somehow. Who knows what these animals are capable of?" Gareth shrugged.

"Are you sure they're just holding dad and the others prisoner and they haven't actually killed them?" Alison had been talking to someone from the Alliance in an attempt to create her cover, but her contact was so distant, so cold, that she couldn't get a read on him. She was told that their entire race was made up of dangerous killers, but she hadn't been able to gather any real evidence of just how ruthless they could be.

"We don't know anything for sure. But it would make sense for them to try and squeeze him for information first. That gives us a little time before they realize he won't talk." Gareth ran his hand over his tightly cropped hair. He looked a lot like their dad when he did this.

"Shit. Well, how the hell will we find out where they're keeping him?" Alison wondered aloud.

"That's up to you, isn't it? You've got to find out where their base is."

Alison rested her face in her hands. *Damn.* "Did you guys *have* to capture one of theirs? This would have never happened if you hadn't taken the girl," Alison argued, tears welling up in her eyes.

"In case you forgot, they got awfully close to us thanks to the information *you* gave them!" Gareth retorted and crossed his arms. Alison hated it when he did that; when he gave her that cocky look like he knew everything.

"I had to give them something, otherwise how would I earn their trust?" Alison asked.

"Did you have to give them the message board, though? A lot of the guys feel that that cut awfully close to home."

"I can't be posing as an informant, if I don't *inform*, can I? And it was you who made the first move to meet with her. You could have just kept her at arm's length and they would have given up sooner or later." Alison felt the anger take over.

Her brother had never taken her particularly seriously. In fact, he probably hated that their dad had chosen her to get close to the Alliance by posing as an informant in the first place. Well, too bad for him. Dad had trusted her to get the job done, not him.

"Still, you're playing a dangerous game with these people, and now we're facing the consequences."

"I've done whatever was asked of me. You can take your hindsight and stick it somewhere."

Alison and Gareth stared at one another, neither in the mood to back down.

"If you've done such a great job at earning their trust, how come you've only ever met one of them? How come you don't know where their base is or even what their full names are?"

"This stuff takes time. Patience. Not that you would ever get that through your thick skull. And plus, our guys were no match for them at the warehouse. Don't you think we ought to arm ourselves a bit better before we can even think of acting?"

"Well you better hope it doesn't take too long, or we'll never get Dad and the others back. As for weapons, they're on the way. Don't you worry about that."

Alison gave him a dirty look and picked up her bag. If she had to stay here with Gareth one more minute, she'd be tempted to clobber him over the head with something. Such was her relationship with her brother – he really knew how to push her buttons.

Wallet, phone, all was in place, so she zipped up the top and threw the strap over her shoulder, ready to make a quick escape when her phone rang, stopping her in her tracks while she checked who it was.

Aidan.

"Keep quiet, it's them," Alison warned her brother, who still had a disapproving scowl on his face.

"Hello?" Alison answered the call.

"Alison. It's Aidan."

"Hello, Aidan. What's going on?" Alison asked, while keeping her eyes glued on Gareth.

"We've made some progress in our investigation and I've been asked to bring you in to see if you can shed some light on a few things..."

"Bring me in?" Alison repeated.

"Yeah. I'll text you the directions. It's time we had a more formal chat, what do you say?"

"Sure. Fine. I'll be there." Alison hung up and stared at her phone for a moment while she collected her thoughts. "They're bringing me in," she said triumphantly when she looked up at her brother again.

"So?" Gareth asked.

"So it seems they *do* trust me sufficiently now. Fingers crossed this goes well and we can get Dad back soon." Alison grinned and looked down at the flickering screen.

One new message. She was to meet Aidan in half an hour, at a park only a couple of blocks from the cafe where they'd met last time. He would take her the rest of the way.

Gareth didn't comment, and Alison didn't wait for him to. She had already been ready to leave before the call, and now she definitely didn't feel like sticking around. She'd grab a bite to eat, then head to the meeting point as instructed by Aidan.

Perhaps she still had a chance to fix things.

———◆———

Alison reached the meeting point ten minutes early and spent the time sitting on a park bench, watching the world go by. It was cold, but she was well prepared and didn't mind the fresh air. Today was a rather ordinary late October day, and Edinburgh's inhabitants as a whole didn't seem to care about the chilly weather either.

Mothers pushed buggies with small children. A group of construction workers passed by her bench on their way further into the park to eat their packed lunches. Of course they couldn't hold back the obligatory inappropriate remarks once they noticed her.

All of these people acted like everything was fine. It wasn't their fault, obviously, nobody had told them about the threats that lurked in the city - and everywhere else in the world for that matter. They had no idea about werewolves, and other dangerous creatures that could attack at any moment. They had no reason to fear the dark.

Alison knew better though, thanks to her dad and his work with the Sons. All their lives, she and Gareth had been taught about the various monsters that threatened humanity. Wolves, bears, lions. These were the three types they knew about, but it wasn't too farfetched to consider that perhaps there were other kinds of hybrids too.

The one thing Alison was certain about was that they were all predators and that human society was no place for them to reside.

She felt herself grow a little jittery, like she normally did shortly before her meetings with Aidan. She wasn't sure which of the three shifter species he belonged to, though she suspected he was a bear due to his impressive height and build. Either way, she wasn't fooled by his calm and controlled exterior.

Most were-creatures were savage animals unable to control the urge to kill. That's what her dad had told her. And that made Aidan a dangerous exception.

"Alison." Aidan's familiar voice interrupted her dark thoughts and made her flinch slightly.

"Hey." She jumped up, not to greet him per se, but more because seeing him tower over her bench put her in too much of a disadvantage if anything were to go wrong.

"Ready?" he asked. "Please give me your phone." Aidan held out his hand.

Alison nodded, and did as asked. He switched the mobile off, opened the back cover and removed the battery just like he'd done before earlier meetings. After he put all of the separate components into his pocket, he gestured at her to follow him out of the park.

They barely spoke while they walked, but Alison couldn't resist the urge to pry.

"So you said you've made some progress?" she asked, while trying to keep up with Aidan's long strides.

"That's right." He looked down at her, probably considering exactly how much information to share with her. "One of our own was taken, but we got her back. With interest."

Alison nodded and kept quiet. Aidan wanted to be vague, and that was fine. Today he was going to bring her into the Alliance hideout, and that was already a massive step in the right direction. Alison didn't want to push her luck.

"How about this weather, eh?" Alison attempted a bit of small talk.

"Mhm." Aidan looked left and right, then scanned the area behind them. "You weren't followed, were you?" he asked finally.

"No. Who would follow me?" Alison asked. God, she hoped Gareth hadn't actually followed her. That was exactly the sort of thing that could ruin her cover.

"All right." Aidan started to walk again and Alison followed, through the narrow alleyways in the old town. Left, right, zig-zagging around the historic buildings, until finally they made it to the other end of the city where the buildings started to look more modern.

Perhaps he had been trying to confuse her, so that she wouldn't remember the route they'd taken. That wasn't going to work, though, Alison thought. She'd lived in Edinburgh for most of her life, ever since her family had moved here when she was just seven years old. She knew this part of town like the back of her hand and no matter how much they walked in circles, she would know exactly how to get to where they were going.

Plus, unless he blindfolded her, she would be able to read the street signs and remember the landmarks.

After walking around seemingly aimlessly for about fifteen minutes, he led her further away from the center of town and towards the harbor. The streets no longer featured pretty old buildings, but bland warehouses and offices, most of which had been constructed in the sixties and seventies. A lot of this area was empty, abandoned. It was the ideal location for a hideout.

Finally, they reached their destination. An old warehouse that didn't stand out in the least. It was as rundown and dilapidated as all the others in the area. The paint was flaking off the woodwork, and weeds made their home in the cracked concrete of the facade. Bingo.

Aidan knocked and waited, though not very long, until the door was unlocked from the inside and swung open.

It was dark inside, and it took Alison a moment before her eyes adjusted to the low lighting. Inside stood a man, at least as tall as Aidan, if not slightly taller. The sight of him took Alison's breath away. He was gorgeous, and also a little familiar...

It was the eyes that got to Alison the most. A pair of almost sparkly blue eyes that pierced the darkness. She couldn't shake the sense of déjà vu. Where had she seen those same eyes before?

The man opposite her was frozen in place as they stared at one another, until what felt like minutes later Aidan cleared his throat, breaking the silence and dragging both of them back into reality.

"Err, I'm Jamie Abbott. You must be Alison Carter."

Alison reluctantly accepted Jamie's outstretched hand. As soon as their fingers touched, a jolt of something - excitement perhaps, or nerves - hit her right in the chest. She didn't know why, but was certain Jamie had felt it too. It was difficult not to say something about how strange she felt.

A subtle smile played on Jamie's lips as she let go after their handshake. As if he understood...

CHAPTER THREE

Meeting the human, Alison, for the first time was a huge shock for Jamie. For a moment he wasn't certain if he was actually awake or had somehow found himself in a vivid dream, like the ones that plagued him every night.

That face. Those green eyes and soft feminine curves. Alison was literally the girl of his dreams. As stupid and cliché as that sounded, it was true. She was the girl from the beach, he was certain of it. There was no way that this was a mistake. He'd seen her face every single night for as long as he could remember.

He'd wanted to ask her if she knew him too, but with Aidan around that seemed too weird a question, so he'd just shaken her hand and introduced himself instead. The look on her face had told him that their meeting was significant for her too. Or had he imagined that?

Shortly after he'd regained his composure somewhat, he'd stepped aside and let Aidan and Alison pass him and head upstairs. Luckily Aidan had understood that Jamie wanted him to take lead on this after all. Jamie found himself sitting opposite the radiant redhead in their newly set up interrogation room. The harshness of the fluorescent light overhead made her hair light up like it was on fire. He was glad that he didn't have the best view of her feminine curves while she sat there, half-obscured by the table, or he'd have even more trouble concentrating.

Aidan asked the questions Jamie had come up with earlier, and Jamie observed. He caught himself staring at her so intently that his eyes burned from forgetting to blink.

He looked down at his right hand which rested in his lap. It was warm where her fingers had touched his. Like they were still touching.

What did it mean? Had he lost his mind?

"Could you tell us again how you found out about those websites you mentioned to me before?" Aidan asked. His tone indicated that he wasn't expecting much of an answer, but Jamie didn't care.

He wasn't sure he wanted to know how she knew either. He just wanted to hear her voice as she answered.

"I worked part time for a hosting company a while back. Tech support. They had some issues with their software which I sorted out. That's how I found out," Alison responded.

Her voice sounded clear yet melodious, like she was singing her answers, not speaking them. He'd definitely lost his mind. Perhaps the years he'd been suffering from insomnia were finally catching up with Jamie.

"Those websites are quite vague to the untrained eye. How did you know that you'd found something worth sharing?" Aidan looked up from the list of questions, scrutinizing Alison.

Jamie tried to read her body language, but he kept getting stuck on tiny, irrelevant details. The dimples in her cheeks. The freckle on the tip of her nose. Her curvaceous lips which begged to be kissed...

"While sorting out their issues, I gained access to the private messaging system," Alison said. She glanced over in Jamie's direction.

Yes, she felt it too. Jamie could tell.

He knew for sure that she was the girl he'd dreamed about as recently as perhaps twelve hours ago. But did that automatically mean that she was also the same girl he'd actually talked to on that beach so many years back? How could he be certain? He had to ask her, but not with Kyle's comprehensive video surveillance system running in the background.

"What did you learn exactly?" Aidan asked.

"That they're dangerous. They want to hurt people."

"What people?" Aidan pushed.

"I'm not sure. The words they used are confusing. Animals. Monsters. I figured they're a bunch of crazy fanatics." Alison blinked a few times, then focused her green eyes on Jamie again.

He couldn't look away. He could barely breathe.

"How about we take a break, huh?" Aidan suggested, while picking up and straightening out the papers with his questions and notes.

Jamie nodded without even looking in his direction, and Alison leaned back in her chair, relaxing visibly as she folded her arms across her chest. With Aidan leaving the room, this was Jamie's chance to talk to Alison. Unfortunately he still had to deal with the cameras Kyle had installed everywhere somehow...

"Can I get you a coffee?" Jamie asked.

Alison looked up at him but didn't reply. Her eyes locked onto his and he was lost. They would have sat there opposite each other, just staring at one another indefinitely if Jamie's phone hadn't broken the spell.

He stole a glance at the screen. Damn. "I'm sorry, I need to take this. I'll be right back," Jamie mumbled, while getting up and rushing out the door, leaving Alison behind. Of all the times for his superiors at the Alliance to phone up, they had to pick this exact moment. Typical.

"Hello?" he answered.

"Abbott. Any progress?" the strict voice on the other end demanded. Alliance council member Adrian Blacke had never been one for small talk.

"The prisoners have kept their mouths shut. We're questioning another lead right now, the human who gave us the websites." Jamie felt his heart rate go up as he thought about Alison. It was his duty to report on what they were up to, but if it were up to him, he'd rather keep Alison's presence a secret. Thanks to his own demand to have video in place in the new interrogation room, he didn't have that option anymore. Blacke would see the footage sooner or later.

"I see. We will send in someone to take those prisoners off your hands within the next 48 hours. You're not equipped to keep them there, and if they're not talking to you anyway, perhaps we'll have more luck."

"But... we're not done questioning them yet," Jamie interjected.

"You have two days. That's all," Blacke said. With that, the conversation was over. The decision to transfer the prisoners had already been made and there was nothing Jamie could do or say to change that.

At least they didn't want to take over Alison's interrogation as well. Yet.

Jamie was still agitated when he slipped the phone back into his jeans. Coffee, that's what he needed.

He headed down the hall and through the door at the end, locking it behind himself, then rushed down the stairs leading down to the office. Aidan was already there and nursing a cup of the steamy hot liquid while going over some of the video footage with Kyle.

"How about the other angle, show me the other angle," Aidan remarked, leaning in closer as Kyle complied with his request. This could take a while. Good.

Jamie stuffed a couple of packets of sugar and creamer into his pocket and emptied the remaining coffee waiting in the coffee maker into two mugs. Then he headed back up the same way he came without disturbing any of the others. He had to get back to Alison, and learn whatever he could before Aidan cut his break short.

Back upstairs, he opened the door to the interrogation room and was relieved to find Alison exactly where he'd left her. Not that she would have had anywhere else to go.

"I wasn't sure how you take it, so here you go," Jamie said, placing the mug as well as the packets he'd brought in front of her on the table.

"Thanks," Alison whispered.

That voice... It made the hairs on Jamie's arms stand up straight, but in a good way.

He watched as Alison fixed her coffee. She had the most elegant fingers, like a concert pianist. He couldn't stop staring at her, she was mesmerizing to watch.

Alison took a first, tentative sip and closed her eyes.

What could Jamie say to her? How could he get her out of this room without raising any suspicion? And if he did, how could he resist the urge to let his inner bear claim her right then and there?

Jamie cleared his throat and Alison looked up from her mug. "This is a bit awkward, so I'm just going to come right out with it," he mumbled.

Alison blinked, waiting for Jamie to continue. He had to force himself to look away or he was convinced his words would come out jumbled up in the wrong order. *Focus, or she'll say no.* He had to make sure his question would at least make some sense.

"I was wondering if you'd like to have dinner sometime." Jamie held his breath while she seemed to mull things over. It was as though time had stood still and the ability to breathe had left him.

She bit her lower lip for a painful few seconds. "Sure," Alison said at last, to Jamie's relief. "I'd like that." She shot him a quick smile that seemed to make everything better.

"Brilliant. Here, take my number. Aidan has yours, I gather?" Jamie said, while sliding one of his business cards over to her. That was the first hurdle done with.

"Yeah, he does." She'd barely finished answering him, when Aidan opened the door, ready to continue.

Jamie sat back, calmer now, knowing that after today's questioning, he'd have the chance to see Alison again in a much more intimate setting. Perhaps then he'd be able to find the answers to all the questions that had plagued him since her appearance on his doorstep earlier.

Aidan shuffled his notes, looking at which question he'd left the conversation at earlier, and proceeded to ask Alison whatever else was on his sheet. A lot of the questions were rephrased repeats of the ones asked earlier, designed to catch her out if she wasn't being truthful. Tedious, but necessary.

Throughout the rest of the afternoon, Jamie continued to sit quietly at the table, watching her answer everything as best she could. She was so patient, so helpful, it was almost surprising. A lot of people might have gotten frustrated at the amount of detail Aidan asked for over and over, but not her.

She was perfect.

When the last question had been asked, Aidan shot him a quick glance and raised his eyebrows to check if he had anything to add. Jamie just shook his head. They were done for now.

Whatever else he needed to get from Alison, he'd get on his own time, without the additional set of eyes and hidden lenses pointed at the two of them.

CHAPTER FOUR

The interrogation had been intense for Alison, and yet... The answers had rolled off her tongue easily and she thought she'd appeared confident and honest and above all, genuine. The thing was, she'd also shared a lot more than she initially planned to.

Such was the effect Aidan's boss, Jamie, had had on her.

Where did she recognize him from? While walking back with Aidan, who again took a convoluted route leading away from the office, probably in an attempt to confuse her, she couldn't get Jamie out of her head.

It had all seemed so simple before: she was going in to give them some vague answers, while memorizing as much as she could about the office and the people within. Despite Aidan's best efforts, she knew exactly where the Alliance building was located and would be able to find it again in a heartbeat.

The next step was to take all that information and hand it over to her brother so that he could mount a rescue for their dad and the other two guys.

The last thing she'd expected was to get a dinner invitation from the Alliance leader. And why the hell had she accepted? Things were simple no longer.

He seemed to be taken with her, so much so that he didn't interfere or interrupt her even once when she was answering Aidan's questions. He only listened, observed. It was as though he felt bad, putting her in an awkward position like that. There was something more to Jamie Abbott, and Alison needed to find out what.

Perhaps it was lucky then that she'd see him again. Her fingers closed around the business card he'd given her. She fished it out of her pocket and held it up to her nose. It smelled of him, strange as it seemed. Like an expensive cologne, but one she'd never had the pleasure of coming across before. Sweet, heady, sexy.

If Aidan was a bear, then Jamie must be one too. They looked similar enough.

Was she really going to go on a dinner date with a werebear? How utterly ridiculous. That was a risk Alison normally would never take, and yet she couldn't have refused. What if he only wanted to lure her out on her own to capture her too? No, if they'd wanted to confine – or worse, kill - her they could have just gotten it over with right there in that creepy little room where they'd questioned her.

Instead they'd let her go on her merry way afterward.

Now that she was alone again, back in the park where Aidan had picked her up a good four hours earlier, she didn't know anymore what she was going to do. Her brother needed two things to rescue their dad: weapons, which would arrive soon enough, and Alison's help in locating the prisoners.

Gareth was out for blood. He wouldn't ask questions, just shoot on sight if anyone opposed him.

There would be casualties, a lot of them. The Sons would strike hard, and aim to reduce the Alliance numbers by any means necessary. Both Aidan and Jamie would be in real danger. The more she thought about it, the more uneasy she grew over the prospect of another confrontation.

Earlier she might have worried about the two men in her life and whether they'd survive the fight. But now, another concern played on her mind more: Jamie's safety.

She couldn't give Gareth the location, at least not yet.

Alison wasn't sure how long she'd sat there thinking things through, but she was no closer to clarity. It had gotten dark in the meanwhile; time to head back home. She reluctantly got up from the park bench and started walking on autopilot.

Soon after, she reached her flat and came face-to-face with a furious Gareth as soon as she'd unlocked the door.

"Where the fuck have you been?" he demanded.

"You know where." Alison dumped her things on the sofa, but as she was heading towards the bathroom, Gareth held her back by her arm.

"You've been gone for hours. No updates, your phone is dead, what the hell am I supposed to think?"

"They made me switch it off," Alison explained, realizing that possibly she should have remembered to switch it back on after they'd let her go, but Gareth didn't need to know about the time she'd spent reflecting on things at the park.

"Well? Where is their base?" Gareth asked.

Alison straightened her shoulders, hoping a more confident posture would make her seem more believable.

"They shifted the meeting elsewhere at the last minute, so I don't know yet. But I do have some good news." Alison wasn't sure whether to be all that candid with her brother, who no doubt would get even more agitated at what she was about to say, but it was all she had to share. "I met the guy in charge, and he seems to have taken a liking to me and asked me out..."

Gareth was speechless, but only for a moment. "You're joking. Don't tell me you've agreed?"

"Put aside your ego for a moment and think about it — we need more information in order to rescue Dad. I've found a chance to get closer to at least one of the animals who are holding him, and you want me *not* to act on it? Have you lost your mind?" The angrier Gareth made Alison, the easier it was for her to sound convincing and distract from the fact that she was hiding information from him.

She stared him down with her hands on her hips, as he glared back at her with fire in his eyes.

"You're going to get into trouble, you know that? This isn't a fucking game." Gareth shook his head and ran his hand over his cropped hair.

"I will be absolutely fine, if you don't drive me nuts first!" Alison insisted.

"Then at the very least I should be there. Follow you. When is this ridiculous date going to happen?"

"Hell no! I can't be expected to maintain cover with this guy if I have to worry about you and your temper lurking in the shadows behind me. And I don't know yet. He's going to call me."

"Whatever. You're going to get yourself killed or worse at this rate."

Alison wanted to argue more, but bit her tongue. At least Gareth had backed off somewhat from the idea of spying on her date, and if she fought on, she might say something she'd regret later. If Gareth got wind that she was keeping stuff from him, she would be in a world of trouble.

"Clearly you're going to do whatever you want to, but keep your goddamn phone on when you meet this guy, all right?" Gareth grumbled.

Alison nodded, and watched as he picked up his leather jacket and headed for the door. *Good riddance.* She needed time alone to think about how she was going to fix things.

———— ◆ ————

As it turned out, Alison didn't get much of a chance to mull her situation over after all. Shortly after Gareth left, she received a phone call from Jamie who suggested drinks and dinner. The man sure was eager, but Alison knew better than to complain.

Sure, he was supposedly the enemy, but Alison was a woman first and Sons member second. It was hard not to feel flattered to have a guy like Jamie fawn over her and call her just hours after meeting for the first time. She accepted his invitation and immediately started sifting through the contents of her wardrobe to find the perfect outfit to wear.

She wanted to impress him, and she didn't know for sure why. Alison had tried her best to justify her impulses by convincing herself that a successful date would give her a better chance to earn his trust. But she did sort of like him, and she certainly was attracted to Jamie. Perhaps the danger he represented had made him more enticing somehow.

Or perhaps she *had* lost her mind, as Gareth had accused her of earlier.

None of that changed the fact that she hadn't been out on a date in a while, and really could use the boost to her self-esteem. Jamie had been quiet earlier in the afternoon, almost a bit shy and awkward, which seemed unusual for a guy as hot as him. Hopefully that had been the case because Aidan had been there too, and when it was just the two of them, he'd loosen up a bit.

Alison had trouble reconciling her conflicting emotions as she got dressed and made up for her date. She wanted things to go well, because it would help her mission, but she couldn't ignore her ulterior motives.

In the past whenever she'd seen a scenario like this portrayed in movies and TV shows, Alison had not been able to imagine ever being in a situation like that, playing a femme fatale who seduces an enemy, just because it was her job.

She wasn't that type of girl, or so she'd thought. Never mind the fact that she wasn't slim or beautiful enough to play the role, she didn't think she was a good enough actress either. Her aversion to her mark would be written all over her face if she ever found herself in a similar situation. She never once had imagined the possibility of losing herself in the fantasy she was only meant to act out.

Eight o'clock came around and Alison was as ready as she would ever be. She'd chosen a flattering A-line skirt and heels, and a pretty blouse that she felt accentuated her best feature, her cleavage.

Alison's hair had always had a mind of its own so she'd given up on trying to tame it years ago. Tonight also, she had just brushed her curls lightly, and kept them untied. A final check in the mirror, and she was out the door.

She didn't think it wise to give Jamie her home address, so they'd agreed to meet at a pub of his choice. Like most things in the center of town, it was only a short walk away from where Alison lived, so she found herself wandering again the same streets that she'd just traveled earlier.

After what had been a cloudy, rather gloomy day, Alison was surprised to find the skies clear overhead. A sign?

The full moon lit up the streets, giving everything from the damp pavement to the historic buildings a mysterious, magical feel.

Tonight wasn't an ordinary date; it was more meaningful than that.

There was a chill in the air that filtered through Alison's long woolen coat and stung against her legs. The streets looked surprisingly empty for this time of night. Normally you'd find couples walking arm-in-arm, tourists rushing back to their hotels after finishing their sightseeing for the day. Tonight it seemed to be just her and the moon and stars up above.

Alison breathed a sigh of relief when she saw the lit up sign of her destination in the distance and sped up for the final stretch. Her heels clicked loudly against the cobbled pavement with every rushed step. She pushed against the door and felt the warmth of the pub interior try to escape around her as she stepped inside.

There he was. Alison's heart skipped a few beats when she spotted Jamie sitting by himself in one of the booths lining the wall. He gave her a quick wave and she forced a smile. Here goes nothing.

"Hi," she said, offering him her hand while bracing herself for the inevitable jolt that would pass through her as soon as they touched...

CHAPTER FIVE

"Hope you found it okay?" Jamie asked while Alison opened her coat, revealing the outfit she'd chosen for the occasion. She looked breathtaking and smelled even better. Should he say so? Would that be too much of a cliché?

"I'm a local, remember?" Alison remarked with a smile that brightened up the entire room.

He'd felt uneasy about the date before she'd arrived, but all his concerns had melted away once in her presence.

"Of course, yes," Jamie mumbled. "Can I order you anything while you get comfortable?"

"Whatever you're having looks good to me," Alison nodded at the half full pint of draught beer in front of him. He'd arrived early of course, having been way too restless to stick around either the office or his home. His habit of finding comfort among crowds of strangers was a hard one to kick.

"Sure."

Jamie waved at one of the bar staff, who came over immediately to take his order.

"So I didn't expect you to call me so quickly," Alison teased. The way she looked at him when she'd said it didn't suggest she minded. If anything, she looked rather pleased to be here. Through the varied scents hanging around the place, Jamie couldn't ignore hers. Irresistibly sweet and intoxicating.

"Well... Life's too short to put a good thing off, don't you think?"

The incredibly efficient twenty-or-so guy who had taken his order appeared again with Alison's drink, placing it on the table in front of her. "Can I get ya anything else?" he asked.

Jamie shook his head. "Thanks."

"You're right. Life *is* too short," Alison repeated.

The scent of her arousal was more pronounced the longer she sat in front of him. If Jamie didn't bring up their history now, he'd never manage the presence of mind to do so later.

"I do have to admit, though, that I'm afraid I had a hidden agenda asking you to meet me here..." Jamie said.

Alison cocked her head to the side and folded her hands on the table. Those green eyes staring at him almost made Jamie lose himself again. A deep breath helped him regain focus.

"Applecross Bay, 1995." Jamie paused and observed Alison's reaction.

She pressed her lips together and all the color seemed to drain out of her face. Her eyes darted back and forth between Jamie's and random spots around the room. She reminded him of cornered prey, and although it was in his instinct to always maintain an advantage in any confrontation, he felt uneasy about putting her in this position.

"That's it. That's why you looked familiar," she whispered.

Alison loosened her hands and rested her face in them for a moment, before looking up at Jamie again through the gaps between her fingers.

"I guess that's it then," she said, under her breath.

"What?" Jamie asked. His mind was racing. Although he was certain that he'd been dreaming of her every night since, it was still a shock to hear her admit that she'd been there. He hadn't lost his mind after all.

"The game's up, eh?" She blinked a few times and

Jamie could see that her eyes had glazed over slightly.

She was visibly upset, and although he should be furious that this woman had had anything to do with what had without a doubt been the very worst day of his life, he couldn't muster anything other than sympathy. She'd been only a child back then, like him.

Jamie reached across the table, resting his hand on top of her arm. To ignore the intense attraction he had for her, especially while touching her was a tall order, but he managed to suppress it somehow. "Alison."

She sniffled and reached into her handbag, retrieving a pack of tissues with her free hand. After struggling to get one out of the wrapper, she dabbed the corners of her eyes with it.

"I can't explain it, I should be angry. I should demand answers. I should... I don't know. Really, I just want to know what happened," Jamie whispered.

"And I should be scared right now," Alison responded, a thoughtful, though still teary-eyed expression on her face. "But..."

"So let's talk. Figure it out." Jamie gently squeezed her arm, enjoying the warmth as it filtered out of her skin and into his fingertips. It was too easy to touch her, so tempting to do so much more...

"He's safe, you know. Your little brother. I don't know where he is now, but he's safe," Alison whispered.

"Matthew. That was his name. We used to call him Matty." Jamie took Alison's hand, threading his fingers through hers. He hadn't said his brother's name out loud in years, it had hurt too much. For some inexplicable reason it felt good to open up to *her* of all people.

"I know. Matthew." A lone tear ran down her cheek as she looked up from their entwined hands resting on the rugged wood of the table. "It was Dad's idea. I had no choice but to go along."

"I know. It's okay," Jamie tried to comfort her. His own pain paled in comparison to the regret and guilt emanating from her. It was heart wrenching, to sense her emotions so keenly.

"It was all part of an experiment. You see, Dad was convinced that every child is born innocent, and if introduced to the right sort of surroundings at an early age, they'd grow up exactly the same as any of us. Matthew was one of the first," Alison explained. "And my name isn't really Carter, it's Campbell."

Alison tried to pull her hand back, but Jamie couldn't bear to let go. "But then your name isn't really Abbott either, is it?" Alison asked.

"No. It's not. I didn't want anyone to look up my history when I joined the Alliance. Whatever happened in the past, it's none of their business." Jamie looked away and pinched the bridge of his nose to ward off another one of his persistent headaches. "Campbell... Any relation to-"

"Lee Campbell. He's my dad," Alison interrupted.

As huge as that revelation was, it didn't surprise him. They looked at each other in silence for a few seconds.

"When I get back to the office in the morning, am I going to find him where I left him?" Jamie asked.

Alison bit her lip, hard. "I haven't told anyone. I was supposed to, but I just couldn't. It doesn't make any sense."

In a way, it made a lot of sense to Jamie. She hadn't been able to do her job and reveal the location of the Alliance building, just like Jamie knew he wouldn't be able to reveal Alison's real identity to anyone within the Alliance. He'd rather take a knife and slit his own throat than to betray her. That could only mean one thing...

The more he thought about it, the more things fell into place, and it also explained why he hadn't been able to get her out of his head ever since that first meeting twenty years ago. They were fated. Back then he hadn't been able to shift yet, so he couldn't sense the connection as strongly as he did now, but his inner bear had seen her once and the memory had never left him alone. They were meant to be.

"What do you know about us?" Jamie whispered and leaned across the table. It was difficult being so close to her, surrounded by her scent, without taking things further, but he didn't want his eagerness to startle her.

"Only what I've been told. That you're half man, half animal. That human morality doesn't apply to you, only animal instinct."

Jamie let out a chuckle. "That latter part isn't quite true, but all right."

"Sometimes you turn into... a bear?" Alison asked, her eyes wide with either curiosity or apprehension. Perhaps a bit of both.

"Yeah. A bear. Let me guess, you people watch Wolf as a documentary?" Jamie joked. "True, we feel certain instincts a lot more keenly than ordinary humans do, but we're not immoral or out of control. Well perhaps in *some* scenarios we like to let go a bit... If you get my drift. But we don't go around killing people indiscriminately."

"It's hard to know what to believe. Most people don't even know you exist. I can't go to the library and do research, except in the horror section."

"Fair point. But then that's because when people do find out about us they tend to pick up their torches and pitchforks..." Jamie grinned.

Alison pulled away and folded her arms, scowling at him.

Jamie regretted teasing her so much, but he couldn't help it. It had been the only thing he could think of to try to cheer her up. At least she'd stopped crying.

"I'm sorry. It's just hard to know truth from fiction," Alison remarked.

"I'm sorry too. I'm not being fair to you. You're taking all this very well, I must say." Jamie smiled at her, and felt his excitement surge to new levels when she reluctantly smiled back.

"All this stuff you feel right now, there's a reason for it..." Jamie started. "I feel it too."

"Oh?"

"It's one of the main differences between us and humans, save for the turning into an animal bit. Our relationships work a bit differently than yours. When a bear finds his mate, they connect on a deep, almost subconscious level."

"Is that what this is? Does it ever fade?" Alison's eyes widened and Jamie was once again shocked at how green they were.

"Bears mate for life," Jamie replied.

"This is insane. I feel like I could wake up any moment now and find that all of it has just been a crazy dream." She picked up her glass and took a big sip.

"I know. We should hate each other, instead we're sitting here, having a pleasant chat over a couple of beers..." Jamie smiled at her, hoping she'd reciprocate. He ached to see her smile again.

"I feel like I want to do more than chat," Alison whispered, then covered her mouth as though she was surprised she'd actually said that.

Jamie let out a laugh loud enough that some of the people seated nearby turned to see what was going on. Her body's visceral reaction to his presence had been obvious to him from the start, but she had no way of knowing that of course.

"Oh believe me, I know what you mean." Every fiber in his body yearned to get close to her. To feel her skin against his...

He could barely take it anymore. Something had to be done or his heart would explode out of his chest.

Alison kept her eyes fixed on Jamie as he got up from his seat and joined her on her side of the table. She didn't protest as he slid his hand around the back of her neck and leaned in, drinking in her scent before allowing his lips to touch hers.

"Wow," Alison breathed, then wrapped her arms around his shoulders and returned his kiss with a deeper, even more passionate one.

It was as though all the fuses in Jamie's mind blew all at once. If they hadn't been out in public, he would have ensured that their clothes would come off that very moment, in shreds most likely. A warm feeling overwhelmed him that was so unusual, alien, that he couldn't identify it at first. Then he realized its meaning: after twenty years of yearning after the same woman during every one of his sleepless nights, he'd found his home.

Jamie pulled back, and gazed into those familiar green eyes once more.

"Now what do we do? About the others, I mean," Alison asked.

"Honestly? I'll be damned if I know." What could they do? To say that both sides would be unhappy about their pairing was putting it lightly. At the same time he knew that this was just the start for them. There was no way he'd let her go after waiting all this time. "I guess we'll have to be careful. How good are you at keeping secrets?"

Alison pressed her lips together, all the while maintaining eye contact. It was as though with that first kiss, the remaining distance between them had been bridged, permanently. She wanted him as he wanted her, he could see it in her eyes. The time for talk had passed.

Let's go then, Jamie thought.

Alison couldn't hide her surprise at hearing him in her head, but quickly recovered and nodded. She was ready.

CHAPTER SIX

This was not how Alison imagined her evening would go. Not at all.

She glanced up at Jamie, who'd rested his arm around her shoulder as they walked, protecting her from the winds that had grown even colder during the short time they'd spent at the pub together. None of it made any sense. He was meant to be the enemy. She was supposed to fight the shifters, not go home with one of them.

And yet, she couldn't help herself. Her hormones, or whatever it was that made her feel this way about Jamie had overridden her capability for rational thought.

He'd tried to explain it to her, the connection bears form with their mates, but she still didn't quite understand how it worked. If it was a bear thing, why did she feel it too? She should turn around and run, to leave him behind and never look back, but she couldn't. It was as though she no longer had a choice in the matter. Her decision making privileges were revoked indefinitely.

Her brother would be furious. She couldn't imagine what her dad would say.

In fact, she should be upset as well. After all, it was her life that was being affected the most. But as she walked through the dark, empty streets alongside the powerful half-man, half-bear that was Jamie, she was actually happy. She felt the glances of the occasional passerby, intimidated by Jamie's presence and it filled her with pride to be his. For him to be hers.

Sure, they'd only just kissed, but it hadn't been like any other first kiss she'd shared with a new lover. She had never felt this way. She had never had this sense of belonging, this feeling of complete and utter safety, like the man she was with would walk through hell and back to protect her.

Jamie would.

She shivered against the cold and his arm drew her against him tighter. Alison closed her eyes and drank in his scent. The same perfume that had clung to the card he'd given her earlier that day, only stronger and more overwhelming.

They were getting close to their destination, she could tell by the way his steps sped up. He was eager to get her home. In the crudest of terms she knew he was eager to get in her pants, and she didn't mind at all. She was equally keen to get in his.

It didn't make any sense. But it felt right.

Her heart jumped when Jamie paused in front of one of the terraced Victorian houses that lined the street. He retrieved a bunch of keys and guided her up the front steps. It was nicer than the little new-build flat where she lived. A lot nicer. So much for all the talk she'd grown up with about how shapeshifters lived like animals.

During their short conversation at the pub it had become clear that a lot of what she'd grown up with had just been plain wrong. Just like Aidan hadn't acted like a senseless monster around her during all the times he'd questioned her, neither had Jamie. He seemed to be just a guy. Sure, he'd be a lot stronger than a normal man, but there was nothing too strange about him so far.

Jamie unlocked the wooden front door and switched on the light inside the hall.

"Welcome to my humble abode," he said.

Funny guy. There was nothing humble about the stylish furnishings that greeted her.

As she turned to face him, his hands were already on her. She wanted to close her eyes, but she didn't want to miss out on the view either. His blue eyes seemed to pierce her soul as he looked at her. Nobody had ever looked at her like this. Not Clive, to whom she'd given her virginity behind the bike shed when she was still in school, or her most recent lover Ian, a Sons member like her dad and Gareth. Nobody.

She shut the door behind them and let out a surprised shriek when Jamie gathered her up in his arms and carried her down the hall. He knew exactly where he was going of course, it was his house, and she could very well guess.

The bedroom was as nice as the rest of the house, a large wooden bed standing proudly in the center of the room. The sheets, curtains, everything matched as though it had been chosen by a professional decorator. But he didn't care about keeping things tidy, just deposited her in the middle of the bed and climbed on top, kicking his shoes off as an afterthought.

She understood now, this is was but a taste of what lay ahead. The one scenario in which bears apparently like to *let go*.

"What's funny?" he asked, leaning down to nibble on her lip.

Alison grinned against his lips. "I'm beginning to see how having a strong animal instinct can come in handy."

"Just you wait, I'll show you animal instinct."

She could do little more than giggle as he got to work on her clothes, unzipping her skirt and tugging it off her in one swift motion. He did the same with her blouse, flipped her over to rid her of her bra and panties and finally unzipped himself.

"Wait a minute, you're not thinking of keeping all *your* clothes on, are you?" Alison demanded.

He paused for a moment and looked down at himself, then at her naked form in front of him on the bed. "All right, all right."

She turned onto her back again and observed as he undressed. Everything about him was perfection, from the sculpted abs to the well-pronounced pecs. If it wasn't for the lustful way he looked at her, he was beautiful enough to give any girl an inferiority complex.

Aidan and Jamie had been the only shifters she'd met so far, so Alison had to wonder if they were all this fit.

"To think you were going to hold out on me..." Alison teased and ran her hand over his firm chest.

"In a rush to see and do it all, are we?" Jamie grinned at her, then hooked his arm through the crook of her knee and flipped her over again.

Jamie got on top of her. The heat of his body against her bare back and buttocks made her shiver. He gently pushed her unruly locks out of the way and started kissing and sucking on her neck.

Alison moaned into the pillow. God, he knew exactly what to do to drive her crazy. The stubble on his chin prickled against her skin, giving her goosebumps.

He was right though, she was in a rush. Clearly, so was he. Throughout the short time they'd spent at the pub together, she'd felt her senses heighten to his presence. She'd been attracted to him from the moment she first laid eyes on the man, but what she'd felt while they were talking earlier was way more intense than any attraction she'd ever known.

By the time he'd all but ripped her panties off, she was beyond ready.

He leaned onto one side and ran his other hand all over the soft curves of her body. His erect cock pressed eagerly against her ass cheek while he explored the curvature of her hips, then reached around her side and gently tweaked her nipple between his fingers.

Every touch of his set her alight.

She leaned up onto both elbows, allowing him free reign over her cleavage and breasts. All the while, he continued to lavish every inch of her shoulders with kisses and nibbles.

Then, unwilling to delay the inevitable any longer, he adjusted himself between her legs, spreading her wide and guided his thick cock towards her slick entrance.

"Oh!" Alison exclaimed, as he pushed against her, forcing her open.

He was big. Bigger than she'd ever had. It burned, but pleasantly so when he entered her.

Jamie filled her so entirely, she found herself lost in a haze of pleasure. He wrapped one arm around her waist and lifted her off the bed.

She was utterly helpless in his arms when he started to thrust into her, slowly at first, then faster and faster. His finger found its way around her hips and into her folds from the front. It didn't take him long to locate her clit.

Alison closed her eyes and just hung on. She could hardly move in his iron grip, neither did she need to because he was already doing everything right.

Jamie sped up further, thrusting into her more intensely than before. Her body took everything he had to give without protest. The burn from his initial penetration faded and was replaced by a growing pressure on her G-spot.

She cried out with every one of his strokes as her pleasure rose to new heights.

"You're the most beautiful woman I've ever seen," Jamie whispered against the back of her neck, sending shivers down her spine all over again.

"You too. Most beautiful man, I mean. Oh God!" Alison responded, his intense thrusts forcing her to pause after every couple of words.

She couldn't focus anymore, couldn't think. It was as though her mind was wiped clean of anything other than their union. He was completely in control of what was happening to her and she was just along for the ride.

He kept fucking her with deliberate movements, all the while manipulating her clit.

She was there, so close, and he seemed to know it somehow. He could tell.

Jamie pushed her down onto the bed for the finale, grinding into her from behind and getting rid of the last shred of self-control she had left. The pillow muffled her final cry as the sweet relief of orgasm washed over her. Rather than pausing or hesitating, he continued on, releasing his hot seed into her shortly after.

They stayed like that, with him on top of her cradling her in his arms again. Sweaty and sated, hoping to drag out their moment of mutual bliss. Neither of them spoke a word for what felt like an eternity, it would have ruined the moment.

Finally, he slipped off to one side, giving her limbs some rest, though he never let her go.

"You're amazing," Alison mumbled, once she found the energy to talk.

"You are," Jamie responded.

He held her tighter, his breaths slowing further and further until she could tell he'd drifted off to sleep. In another situation she might have minded, she might have felt alone to have a new partner fall asleep so soon after making love for the first time. But somehow, everything was different with Jamie.

She carefully lifted his arm off her and sat up in the bed

to watch him.

Something about him had changed. He didn't look as serious as he did when awake. He looked completely calm and at rest, even the otherwise permanent crease between his eyebrows had smoothed out. Alison wasn't sure how she knew, but this moment was significant. A sign of complete trust.

She could watch him for hours like this, no matter how creepy that sounded. Unfortunately, she didn't get the chance to just yet.

"What's funny?" Jamie said when he opened his eyes only moments later.

"You look so sweet when you're sleeping." Alison grinned down at him.

"I didn't sleep!" Jamie protested, and sat up himself.

"Yeah. Sure."

"Really!" Jamie insisted. "Anyway, this is unacceptable. I asked you out for dinner, didn't I? I'd better keep my promise."

Alison watched as he got up from the bed and found some takeaway menus in the bedside table.

"Pizza?" Jamie asked, with an apologetic frown on his face. Perhaps he'd wanted to take her somewhere nice, but they'd been so preoccupied with one another, they hadn't noticed the time. It was too late to go out now and besides, Alison didn't want to leave.

"Perfect," Alison said.

Jamie took the menu and left the room to place the order, leaving Alison alone with her thoughts for a moment.

What a night.

In the span of just a few hours, she'd gone from confused about the idea of dating the enemy, to understanding they were soul mates, now and forever. She ought to feel guilty about betraying her family, but somehow, she didn't.

Instead, Alison still felt terrible finding out she'd been instrumental in the abduction of Jamie's brother, Matthew. His capacity for forgiveness in the matter had amazed her. Matthew's disappearance had left a gaping hole in his being. That much was obvious from the way he'd talked about that day. No matter what he said, it was at least in part her fault. She'd do anything to help make things better.

"Done. It'll be here in half an hour," Jamie said, as he came back into the bedroom, phone in hand.

"Really. I wonder how we will pass the time," Alison teased, while obviously checking out his naked body from head to toe.

That was all the encouragement Jamie needed to get back into bed.

CHAPTER SEVEN

It was just another late morning at the Alliance office. Two days had passed since Jamie's first date with Alison, and although he'd made no real progress questioning the prisoners no matter how hard he tried, Jamie felt invincible.

He and Alison hadn't been able to stay away from each other and had spent every spare hour together. Gone were the days when Jamie didn't know what to do with himself once his working day was over.

Gone also were the sleepless nights, the endless restlessness and unnerving dreams that threatened to spill over into reality. He was a changed man, who no longer lived to work, but worked to live.

"What time is the pick-up?" Jamie asked Kyle, who had been coordinating with their contact at the Alliance Council.

"Depending on traffic on the M1, probably early afternoon," Kyle said, without looking up once from his computer screen.

Kyle was the odd one out at the office. Not only was he a black bear unlike Jamie and Aidan who transformed into brown bears, he was a bit of a nerd and awkward around people, especially women. His pale complexion stood out against the darker hair, a testament that he was less outdoorsy than the others on the team.

Though Kyle could fight if he needed to, his main weapon was his brain and Jamie was thrilled to have him on his side. In fact, perhaps Jamie could utilize Kyle's particular skill set for something of a more delicate nature...

Jamie looked over at Heidi, who was reviewing the tape from Alison's interrogation on her own. Aidan was out running a few errands, which made this one of the rare times Heidi and Aidan weren't joined at the hip. She was distracted, so Jamie decided to pull Kyle aside for a private chat.

"Kyle, a moment?" Jamie waved at him, then opened the bottom drawer of his desk and picked up the brown cardboard dossier he always kept in there.

"Sure. What's up?" Kyle approached Jamie's desk.

Jamie handed him the file. "This one's off the books, but I would appreciate if you could look into this case for me when you get the chance."

Kyle opened it and studied the photographs and reports inside. They exchanged a silent look. He understood. "Sure thing, boss."

Jamie breathed a sigh of relief. Just as he'd hoped, Kyle hadn't demanded an explanation or made things more awkward than they needed to be. Jamie watched him walk back to his computer as if nothing of note had happened.

It was only a matter of hours before they'd lose the prisoners. The Alliance leadership had some bigger plans for them that Jamie wasn't privy to, and it was a professional loss for their office. Perhaps he'd take another crack at Lee Campbell in particular. If only the man knew what Jamie had been up to with his daughter for the past two nights, it might wipe that smug grin off his face.

But Jamie didn't get the chance to head downstairs. A loud bang on the door disrupted the calm atmosphere of the office. Was that the transport already? Kyle couldn't have gotten their arrival time that wrong, could he?

"Open up!" An unfamiliar voice filtered through the heavy, reinforced front door.

Jamie jumped up to face the threat, as did Heidi. They exchanged a look, while Kyle furiously typed something into a message window on his computer.

"It's not our people. They're still about an hour away," Kyle whispered, looking up at Jamie with an alarmed frown on his face.

Jamie nodded, then signaled at Heidi to head to the basement. She didn't hesitate for even a second. For all their differences, Jamie had to respect the wolves' ability to follow orders, especially in a crisis. She was out of the room before the second, much louder bang on the door. Jamie waved at Kyle to position himself behind him, who did so after triggering the silent alarm they'd installed as a precaution months earlier.

Seconds later, the door started to creak and splinter under the repetitive impacts typical of the same type of manual battering ram Jamie and Aidan had used during their attack on the Sons' base. Whoever it was, they were determined to get inside and had brought the necessary equipment with them.

"The data!" Kyle shouted, as he sprinted back to his workstation and pulled the hard drive out of his computer. He hid it underneath the false bottom in one of his desk drawers, created just for this purpose.

"Get back, Kyle!" Jamie ordered.

The door swung open, revealing about a dozen determined-looking skinheads in full combat gear. *Crap.* Lee Campbell had been right. It was a counterattack.

"On the ground, filth!" The man in front bellowed, while pointing the muzzle of his weapon in Jamie's direction. If looks could kill... Green eyes, exactly the same shade as the pair Jamie had been gazing into for hours these past few days, shot daggers at him. This must be Alison's brother. *Shit.*

Jamie weighed his options. Should he comply or attempt to fight? They were outnumbered and outgunned. Shifters didn't use firearms, they rarely had the need to because of their greater physical strength compared to regular humans. Then again, large scale confrontations between the two were rare because both sides kept such a low profile.

There was no point to endanger Kyle and himself unnecessarily. Jamie grudgingly got down onto the ground and placed his hands behind his head. Kyle followed his example next to him.

"Good. Cuff 'em," the man ordered and one of his companions stepped ahead and reluctantly placed steel handcuffs around Jamie's wrists. From the solid clicking noise they made as they were tightened, Jamie could tell they weren't toys and would be impossible to break free from without help.

"Up on your feet," Alison's brother barked. "Tell us where you're holding our brothers, animal!"

Jamie got up and stared down at the man in silence. If they hadn't brought guns, this much shorter human would have been no match in hand-to-hand combat, even for Kyle.

"Don't worry, we have ways of making you scum talk." The man gave him a hateful look, then focused his sights on Kyle. "You. You tell me where they are!"

Kyle also didn't say a word.

Jamie knew how this would play out. Their silence would buy a little time, but these people would soon find their prisoners down in the basement on their own. Guarded only by Heidi, who also didn't carry a gun, they'd have no trouble freeing them.

After that, there was no way of knowing what these guys would do. The Alliance attack had resulted in two deaths, mainly because the humans hadn't known when to surrender. This strike was probably as much about revenge as rescuing their men, so once they'd found the cells, they might just kill Heidi, Kyle and Jamie for sport.

"They're alive," Jamie said at last.

Alison's brother shot him another hateful look. "Where? Or do I need to beat it out of you?"

Jamie felt his entire body tense up as instinct tried to take over. *Beat it out of him? Let this clown try.* He tried his best to remain calm, because if he shifted right here in front of a bunch of trigger-happy fanatics, he was certain he wouldn't survive it.

"Fine, have it your way," the man hissed, and stepped up ahead, until he stood right in front of Kyle. He held his weapon to Kyle's temple and turned to make eye contact with Jamie again.

"You tell me what I want to know, or your friend here gets it."

There was no doubt in Jamie's mind that the threat was real. These were the people who had been responsible for disappearances of shifters everywhere, and they'd think nothing of eliminating another one of their enemy.

If Kyle was afraid for his life, he didn't show it. Jamie knew it was over. If he gave up the prisoners, at least hopefully he could ensure Heidi didn't do anything to get herself hurt either.

"Downstairs." Jamie nodded in the direction of the door leading to the staircase.

"Both of you lead the way. Go on." Alison's brother prodded the muzzle of his weapon into Jamie's shoulder blade, forcing him ahead.

One of the armed intruders stepped ahead of them to open the door for Kyle and Jamie, while the rest waited for the two bears to step into the staircase.

"Don't do anything stupid, you hear?" The man warned, prodding his gun into Jamie's back again.

Jamie wasn't planning to. He'd go along with whatever these people wanted, just as long as it would keep his team safe. They went down the stairs into the dark hallway leading to the basement rooms they'd repurposed as holding cells. Heidi was waiting by the first door, tense, ready for confrontation.

"Oh, hell," Heidi said under her breath.

"Stand down," Jamie said, making a calming motion with his hand.

She didn't seem convinced, especially now that the men behind Jamie and Kyle came into view, but didn't argue.

One of the armed men stepped around the two bears, holding another set of handcuffs.

"It's okay, Heidi. Just give them what they want." Jamie watched while Heidi was being restrained.

Some of the other intruders started to fan out ahead, inspecting the doors leading off from the corridor. These rooms originally didn't have windows, so Jamie had ordered Kyle to install spyholes in the doors before securing each prisoner inside. The Sons members now benefited from the same, looking inside first and breaking down only those doors that contained one of their own.

"They're here," one reported, after peeking into the first cell.

Most of his associates scattered around to explore the rest of the rooms, leaving only two guys to guard the three shifters. This was as close to a chance to escape as they'd ever get, but still it seemed too risky to do anything rash.

"How the hell did they find our location?" Heidi whispered. She kept her volume so low, it would have been nearly impossible for human ears to pick up her words, but obviously Jamie and Kyle didn't have that problem.

"No idea," Jamie responded.

"Alison," Kyle mumbled.

Jamie tensed at his suggestion. "No way."

"He has a point. Our position has never been compromised before. Now these people turn up mere days after calling her in? It can't be a coincidence," Heidi remarked.

Jamie felt a red haze descend over his senses. It was an impossibility for Alison to betray him, put him in danger. But he couldn't very well tell these two that, could he? He couldn't reveal how he knew Alison was innocent. It was one thing for two shifters of opposing species to pair up, but a bear and a human? That was almost unheard of.

"I'm not convinced she's given us her real identity. Looking into it, there are precious few records mentioning an Alison Carter that fit her profile." Kyle gave Jamie a thoughtful look.

Jamie balled his fists and took a deep breath to regain his composure. He focused on Kyle again.

"We'll figure it out. But a good investigator rules out other options before being absolutely certain of a suspect's guilt. Remember that," Jamie said.

"Sure thing, Boss." Heidi nodded.

Kyle didn't look convinced, but didn't argue further.

This was a bloody nightmare. With the Alliance pick-up barely an hour out, he'd lost the prisoners. If they couldn't somehow recover the situation, the three of them could be killed. And who knew what the Sons would do with the intel they'd recover from the office eliminating them? This one incident could tilt the fight entirely in their favor.

Once the dust settled on today's events, the Alliance council would no doubt come to the same conclusion as Kyle and Heidi. It wouldn't be so difficult to figure out

Alison's real identity, and that would be the end of it. They'd come after her next.

Something had to be done.

CHAPTER EIGHT

Alison couldn't explain exactly what happened to her at around eleven that morning, but it wasn't good. Her stomach was in knots and even though it was an unseasonably nice, bright day, she felt trapped and skittish under the blue skies. Something was very, very wrong.

Was she coming down with something? Caught a cold, perhaps?

That couldn't explain her paranoia. No, it must be something else.

After pacing around her little flat for a good fifteen minutes, unable to find rest or figure out what she should do with herself, she finally knew she needed a change of scenery. Alison put on her coat and rushed out the door.

While wondering if a walk in the park would do her some good, her feet carried her forward almost involuntarily. She walked on and on until she realized she was getting close to the edge of town, heading toward the neighborhood where the Alliance building was located.

Jamie.

She had to see Jamie. He would know what to do.

Alison's throat felt tight, like an invisible hand had grabbed hold of her and squeezed her tight.

The closer she got, the faster she walked, until she was ready to break into a jog. It was crazy, like one of those dreams in which someone's chasing you. Of course that was silly. No matter how often she looked back, there was nobody in sight.

She was out of breath by the time she reached the door where she'd seen Jamie for the first time. It was shut and there was no sign of activity anywhere in the building. If she didn't know any better, the state the dilapidated warehouse was in would have suggested it was abandoned.

With her heart still pounding in her chest, she took a step back to look up. The windows were boarded up, so she couldn't see inside. *Damn.*

The entrance was offset from the main road in a narrow service alley. Perhaps she'd have better luck on the other side of the building?

Although she wasn't sure what was happening, Alison knew Jamie was in there somewhere. She could sense his presence nearby.

She hurried around the side of the building, turned the corner, and finally found a breach: the front door had been smashed in, the frame left in splinters.

This was Gareth's work. There was no other possible explanation. Somehow, despite Alison's best efforts to blow him off, he'd discovered the Alliance's location on his own.

Alison didn't know what she would find inside. She was unarmed and terrified. If Gareth didn't already know she'd been bullshitting him, he certainly would if she came face-to-face with him after wandering into the Alliance office, proving the fact she had known its location all along. But at least Jamie was still alive. She would have felt it if he wasn't.

Now what? Call the police?

"Hey, what are you doing here?" a familiar voice made Alison jump.

She turned around and found an equally frazzled looking Aidan looking right at her. "Long story. They've been attacked!"

Alison pointed at the broken door and waited while Aidan inspected the damage and peeked inside for a moment. He seemed different, much less stoic and controlled than usual.

"I know. The silent alarm was triggered a short while ago, when I was already on the way back. That doesn't explain why you're here though." Aidan gave her a suspicious look, then glanced back up at the building.

Aidan had never particularly warmed towards her and always seemed a bit suspicious. Turning up at the scene of an attack wasn't helping. She had to find a sensible explanation... Screw it, she had nothing. Jamie had made it clear that the truth wouldn't be particularly popular with anyone, including his own people, but it was the only chance she had of earning Aidan's trust.

"This is going to sound really crazy, but Jamie and I are mates. I felt he was in danger." Alison's bottom lip was trembling while she spoke. She still felt the risk, and if they didn't hurry up, things could get a whole lot worse.

"Okay." Aidan looked away from her again, fished his phone out of his pocket and read something on its screen.

"Really. I know it's not acceptable, considering I'm not one of you, but-"

"Calm down. I believe you."

Wow, that was easy.

"My mate is inside too," Aidan added, looking up from his phone to make eye contact with her.

Finally his demeanor started to make sense. They were in the same boat together. He'd been brought here not by some silent alarm, but the same feeling of uneasiness that had spurred Alison into action. The alarm had just served to confirm the danger he'd already sensed himself.

"So what do we do now?" Alison wondered aloud.

"We're going in, of course! Backup is arriving shortly." Aidan put the phone away, straightened his back and started marching towards the door.

Shit. This was it: the moment of truth. She knew she couldn't do anything to betray Jamie, but Gareth was in there. Despite everything, he was still her brother. Her dad was in there too, more than likely.

She had to pick a side and it would no longer be possible to keep her relationship with Jamie a secret from the rest of them either.

"Wait! What do you mean, *shortly?*" Alison rushed into the building behind Aidan. She wasn't going to be much use in a fight, but considering everything was already unraveling around her, perhaps she could use her position to her advantage.

"Ten minutes, tops." Aidan scanned the empty office space. Wherever Gareth and the guys were, it wasn't in here.

Alison felt Jamie more keenly, and her feet wanted to carry her ahead to his position, making it nearly impossible to focus. Every second they wasted discussing what to do increased the risk of escalation inside. She had to be proactive, and get Aidan on her side.

"I haven't been entirely truthful with you." Alison turned to face Aidan, who paused. "I don't have time to get into it now, but they know me in there. I'm going to stall them, try to get them away from your people if possible. You stay out of sight until the backup gets here and then surprise them."

Aidan's jaw tightened. He wasn't happy to find out she'd played him, but seemed to accept this wasn't the time to argue about it. "Fine. Don't make me regret this. I don't have to tell you what will happen if anything happens to Hei- them."

Aidan's threat didn't faze Alison. If something happened to Jamie, she wouldn't be able to live with herself anyway. "Okay then." *Here goes nothing.*

Alison looked back at Aidan one last time before heading for the door leading out of the cluttered office space. It creaked heavily as she pushed it open, making her flinch. Hopefully nobody had heard her.

She listened for any movement up or down the stairs. She knew that she'd been kept upstairs during her interrogation. That must mean that the prisoners had been locked up downstairs...

Alison tiptoed down the steps until she heard muffled voices, though she couldn't make out what they were saying exactly. There was another door at the bottom of the staircase, which led into a dimly lit corridor.

Alison pushed the door open. Its shrill squeak sent shivers down her spine. There they were. Heads turned in her direction and she recognized the faces of the two armed guards waiting in front of one of the doors leading off the hallway.

"Lads," Alison mumbled.

The two skinheads exchanged a look and then shrugged and nodded at her. So far so good.

"Gareth called me in, where is he?" Alison asked, hoping they wouldn't detect the slight tremble in her voice.

"In there." One of the men gestured at a door further down the hall.

Alison kept her shoulders straight as she marched onward past the pair of them. She managed to steal a glimpse out the corner of her eye at the door they were guarding, but there was no window to see inside. That's where Jamie was, she could feel him. Hopefully he could feel her, too and then he'd know that she was here to help.

Her feet felt like they were made of lead as she forced herself to move ahead, when all she wanted to do was rush inside that first room to make sure Jamie was okay. Assuming there was nobody else inside the room where the Alliance people were held, the current scenario was ideal for a rescue. As long as she could keep most of the Sons out of the way.

Could she risk a quick message to Aidan to let him know? No way, the two geniuses by the door were probably still gawking at her.

She pushed against the door the guards had pointed out to her and was greeted by a half-dozen surprised faces clad in combat gear, along with three in civilian clothing. The room looked depressing, barren except for a bed and mattress. Paint peeled off the ceiling and walls, revealing damp patches in the concrete. This must have been one of the cells where the Alliance had held their prisoners.

"Alison," Lee Campbell said. "What are you doing here?"

She cocked her head to the side, then jumped ahead to give him a hug. "Dad! I'm so glad you're okay."

Tears burned in her eyes. This was an impossible position to be in. Of course she was glad he was unharmed. He was her father. But since the first night with Jamie, he wasn't really her family anymore.

She let out a sob as his arms tightened around her. "It's okay, darling. It takes a whole lot more than a few days of confinement to bring me down!"

"Sis..." Gareth's voice spoke behind her. "What *are* you doing here? How did you know where to find us?"

She didn't move, just sniffled into her dad's shoulder for a moment while considering her answer.

Of all the familiar faces she'd seen coming into the room, one had been missing: her ex, Ian. Perhaps...

"Ian called me, thought you could use some help handling the prisoners. After all, I'd spoken to some of them before," Alison said, while turning around and smiling at Gareth. "Good to see you've got the situation under control."

"Right." Gareth stared at her in silence for what felt like forever, but then turned to face one of the other former prisoners, inspecting the bandage on his leg. "I think we should get Bob, here, to a doctor as soon as possible."

"Can I have a look?" Alison asked. She'd had some first aid training, so it was only natural to ask.

Gareth stepped aside and waved her over. "What do you think?"

Alison's mind was still racing. If she could stall everyone in here until Aidan's backup arrived, perhaps she'd have a fighting chance of defusing the situation without endangering Jamie and the others.

"This might hurt," Alison whispered, as she carefully pulled away the cotton gauze covering some of the man's wounds. His leg was in a bad state, though there was no sign of infection so far and it was starting to heal a little.

"I don't think he should walk," Alison concluded, while making more of a show of inspecting his leg than strictly necessary. He probably could walk without any issue, but it was all she could think of to buy some time.

"Do you think you can use some of those blankets to make a stretcher of some sort?" Alison asked Gareth, who looked at their father for confirmation.

"Really? Can't we just prop him up and let him limp out of here?" Gareth argued.

"He's not bleeding right now, but if it starts we'll have no way of stopping it and he could be in real danger," Alison lied.

"She's right, better safe than sorry," their dad chimed in.

It hurt. He was supporting her in front of Gareth, yet here she was fighting for the other team. Then again, they wouldn't hesitate to kill Jamie if they knew about their affair. And for what? For being a different species?

Alison had to wonder if other than for reasons of vengeance, shifters had ever actually attacked and harmed humans. More often than not it had been the Sons who struck first.

She bitterly remembered the origin story of the Sons that her dad had told her when she was little, about a bear who abducted a human woman to be his bride many centuries ago. The story of Eileen and Bhaltair. The rescue team sent in by the woman's father, Lord Domnall, were the first of what was to become a long line of shifter hunters. But that was just myth, surely?

Since then, had shifters actually done anything wrong? Most of them seemed to live their lives in secret, separate from human society to prevent anyone from knowing the truth about them... Torches and pitchforks were never too far away when shifters revealed themselves as *different*, as Jamie had rightly remarked.

Alison was certain she was now on the right side of this fight, but she didn't want these Sons dead either. She'd grown up with some of them. She observed Gareth and his men fold and arrange the blanket, tearing strips to secure to bits of wood scavenged from what had been a bed frame only moments before. It took them a while, but in the end, they had a makeshift stretcher.

Now what? Alison had started to panic over finding another reason to keep everyone in here when the door finally flung open with a loud crash. The figures that entered didn't belong to the other guards outside. They weren't even human. Aidan's backup had arrived!

CHAPTER NINE

The change in the air had been gradual.

Jamie sat with Heidi and Kyle in a row on the bed, staring at the locked door. If they shifted, it would be no match for the three of them. They could easily break through, but they'd still have to take care of the dozen armed fanatics on the other side. It would be a suicide mission.

While he sat and tried to come up with some sort of a plan to keep his team – and mostly Alison – from any fallout from today's cluster-fuck, what had seemed like a hopeless situation started to change. He felt the change, a presence. It was faint at first but then the sensation grew until he could identify it: Alison.

She was here.

He felt her near the cell, exchanging words with someone outside. If he could feel her through the door, he was certain she could feel him, too. She had come here for him.

His optimism was short-lived as she passed by his cell. She was moving ahead, probably to confront the rest of the Sons who were further down the corridor tending to the prisoners. How would she be able to explain her presence? If they found out why she was really here... He dreaded to think of what would happen.

Jamie tried to listen to the conversation that took place in the other cell after Alison opened the door, but the walls were too thick even for his keen sense of hearing. All he heard were indistinct mumbles.

He couldn't stay still any longer and got up, pacing the

room restlessly.

"You okay, Boss?" Heidi asked, her eyes wide with concern.

She was a sweet girl, loyal to a fault.

"Fine." Jamie paused, listening for any sign of trouble next door, but there was none.

Still, Alison was upset – he could feel it. So he started pacing again.

"Aidan," Heidi whispered behind Jamie.

Had Alison brought him here? Or had he come in after her on his own accord?

"Heidi, I respect your wish for privacy, but if there's anything you can feel that'll help us, please share," Jamie said.

"What?" Kyle wondered aloud.

Jamie shot him a strict look in an attempt to keep him quiet. There was no time to explain.

"He's here," Heidi said, looking up at Jamie. "We'll be okay."

"Is he alone?" Jamie wondered. He knew he was able to communicate with Alison telepathically, but only when they were in the same room together. Perhaps Heidi and Aidan's bond was stronger because they'd been an item for longer.

Heidi closed her eyes and seemed to concentrate, hard. "No. I think the Alliance pick-up has arrived early."

"Shit, really? That's awesome," Kyle exclaimed.

"Get ready," Heidi said.

Jamie cleared his mind, as much as possible with Alison's fear leaching through the wall separating them, and prepared himself. Beside him, Kyle quickly took off his T-shirt.

"What? I don't want to ruin it. They don't sell these anymore," he justified when Jamie gave him a questioning look.

"Five... Four... Three..." Heidi gestured the rest of the countdown.

For the first time since Heidi's rescue, Jamie let the beast out. Ordinarily, he dreaded it. His bear form had always felt painfully incomplete, so he avoided shifting unless a situation absolutely demanded it. Now things were different.

The tickle that traveled the length of his body as brown fur started to break through his skin actually felt pleasant. A burn in his muscles signaled growth. Within a split second, he'd torn through his clothes.

Beside him, Kyle had transformed into his slightly smaller black bear form and Heidi stood on all fours, her razor sharp teeth exposed as she growled at the door. On her signal, they charged ahead, breaking through the door.

Alison. I'm coming.

Jamie lashed out at one of the two armed guards in the hallway, as Heidi and Kyle took on the other. At almost the same moment, a group of bears in varying shades of brown led by Aidan's huge bear form charged through the door coming from the stairwell.

Jamie didn't recognize anyone else, but gladly handed over his slightly bruised prisoner to one of the strangers who had arrived as part of the Alliance Council transport.

"The rest are in there," Jamie said, while leading the way. He had to get to Alison before any of the others did.

"The girl is one of ours," Aidan remarked behind him, giving Jamie pause.

Aidan knew?

Jamie cleared his mind and charged ahead, breaking into a run before crashing through the door.

"What the-" a Sons member on the other side of the door exclaimed.

Two of them carried the wounded guy they'd held prisoner on an improvised stretcher, so they couldn't react without dropping their comrade. The others were scrambling for their weapons.

Jamie went straight for Alison's brother, pinning him to the ground under the immense weight of his paws. Behind him, Aidan, Kyle and Heidi also charged in and neutralized some more of the intruders, growling, biting, and slapping weapons out of their hands, but making sure not to harm them too badly. The Alliance backup did the same until, after just minutes, they had disarmed and surrounded all of the Sons members in the room.

Most of them hadn't even fought back. The element of surprise was a powerful thing indeed.

In the center stood an unarmed man who hadn't been engaged so far: Lee Campbell.

"You didn't think it was going to be that easy, did you?" Aidan snapped at him.

He didn't reply, but he suddenly looked utterly defeated. Gone was the smug prisoner who had taunted Jamie and the others during every interrogation. He'd lost. It seemed as though the man had aged ten years in a span of seconds.

Next to Campbell stood Alison, shivering visibly. Jamie let go of Gareth and stepped up to her. She wobbled slightly, and seemed dangerously close to losing her balance as she looked down at him.

Are you okay? Jamie stretched his paw out in her direction, just in case she needed to steady herself.

I don't know, she responded, pressing her lips together tightly. This was a lot to take in. As much as Jamie and she had shared over the past couple of days, he hadn't transformed in front of her before.

She looked over at Gareth and her dad and tears

started to stream down her face.

"I fucking knew it!" Gareth hissed at Alison, attempting to get up. Heidi pushed him back down with her front paws. "You filthy whore!"

"Watch it," Campbell interjected.

"No, Dad! Enough! While you've been rotting away in this building, your favorite over there has been screwing the enemy!" Gareth groaned as Heidi shifted more of her weight onto his upper torso.

"That can't be. Alison, tell him he's wrong. Whatever you did, you were just doing your job, right?"

Jamie glanced around the room at everyone. Despite being in animal form, their expressions were clear as day. Surprise. Shock. Anger. This was bad.

"That's enough. Let's get them out of here." Jamie attempted to regain control of the situation.

"The girl has been informing for us. She brought me in to coordinate the rescue," Aidan explained.

A few bears Jamie had never seen before exchanged looks, as though they weren't quite convinced by Aidan's words, but nobody argued back.

Heidi jumped into action first, nudging Gareth up and snapping at him when he tried to turn around.

"You're going to pay for this," Gareth growled, while he was forced out of the door.

Reluctantly, Kyle followed suit and got his prisoner up as well, herding him out the room behind Heidi.

One after the other, the guys from the Alliance Council secured the Sons members, using heavy cable-ties as stand-in handcuffs and placing cloth bags over their heads. Jamie stayed behind with Alison and watched them as they led prisoner after prisoner from the room.

When the room was largely empty, a familiar human face entered. Adrian Blacke, wearing one of his trademark black three-piece suits. No doubt he thought his outfits made him look more authoritative.

"I don't have to tell you that we expect a detailed report of what went wrong here," he said to Jamie.

Blacke turned and scrutinized Alison from head to toe. "I suppose thanks are in order for your role in the rescue."

She nodded, but didn't say a word.

"I probably don't need to tell you that what you've seen here today is strictly confidential. Your loyalty will be rewarded. Similarly, if we find that you've breached that confidentiality, there will be consequences."

Jamie glared at Blacke, but quickly reined in his distaste for the man when he turned to face Jamie. "You'll monitor the situation, Abbott. And that report. Monday at the latest, understand?"

Jamie nodded. "Yes, sir."

Blacke stared at him a bit too long for comfort. Aidan and Heidi knowing about Alison were fine, but enough. Even if they disapproved, they wouldn't say a word. Kyle would probably remain loyal as well, but Blacke was dangerous. Jamie had to make sure he never found out the truth about him and Alison.

Who the hell was that? Alison wondered.

Alliance council member, Jamie responded. *Uptight bastard.*

They watched as Adrian Blacke left the room again, leaving the two of them alone. His footsteps faded as he walked down the hall, and back up the stairs where he had originally come from.

I'm sorry it turned out like this, Jamie thought.

No. I'm sorry. I have to conclude that Gareth followed me and I led him right to you. Alison turned to face Jamie again. Her eyes were still moist from crying earlier, causing her lashes to stick together.

He wanted to hold her, tell her it was all going to be

okay. But it wasn't. She'd lost her family today.

Jamie listened for any sounds, but the basement was completely quiet. They were on their own for now.

I'm equally responsible. He could have found this place by following me as well, Jamie thought.

Are they going to hurt them? Alison wondered.

Jamie had no answer. He and his team had never tortured the prisoners, just used basic interrogation techniques to encourage them to talk. Unfortunately Jamie had no way of knowing the lengths Blacke would go to if he thought it could help him extract information.

I'm sorry. Jamie closed his eyes and transformed back into his human self. He wrapped his arms around Alison, who melted into his embrace.

What had started off as an impossible situation for his team had been turned around into a victory. But Alison's loss made it feel hollow.

"I'm so glad you're okay. All morning I've felt like I had this black cloud following me around. Like something terrible was going to happen to you," Alison whispered.

"Really sorry about your dad and brother," Jamie responded, caressing her hair.

She didn't respond straightaway.

"I guess now we're even, huh? A brother for a brother."

Alison's inner turmoil tugged at Jamie's heart. He'd never wanted to get even. All he'd wished for, even after finding out her identity, was to make her happy. Right now that was clearly an impossibility, but maybe one day he'd get another chance.

"Let's go," she mumbled. "You ought to wear something, or people will talk."

Jamie forced a smile. "Don't worry. Nudity isn't as much of a taboo among shifters as it is among humans."

"Uh-huh." Alison wrapped her arms around herself and followed Jamie out of the room.

With a bit of luck, Blacke and his people would have already left, leaving Jamie free to deal only with his own team.

CHAPTER TEN

Alison caught up with Jamie as they reached the bottom of the stairs. Nudity might not be a big deal for him and his people, but if she kept watching his naked behind for much longer, her physical reaction to him would definitely make things awkward in front of the others.

"Aidan knows," Jamie remarked, as he glanced over at her.

"Yeah, I'm sorry. I had to tell him, or he would have never trusted me," Alison explained.

Jamie rested his hand on her shoulder. His hand felt so warm, almost feverish as it burned into her through her clothes. "That's fine. Don't worry about it."

Alison closed her eyes for a moment. She'd felt so torn between the two aspects of herself when everything went down that it had brought tears to her eyes. Deep down she knew she'd done the right thing, but it didn't make things much easier. She took another few steps with Jamie following closely behind.

"Did you know he's with the girl, what's her name? The one Gareth abducted," Alison remarked.

"Heidi? Yeah, I had guessed as much, though neither of them were willing to openly talk about it."

"Why's that?" Alison paused at the top of the stairs, nervous about facing everyone again, so their ongoing conversation was a convenient excuse to delay the inevitable.

"He's a bear, she's a wolf. It's complicated."

"Funny. I would have never thought you guys had issues like that within your ranks."

Jamie smiled at her. "We're a complicated bunch. Anyway – let's go in."

Alison took a deep breath. *Here goes nothing.*

Jamie pushed the door open and Alison flinched at the horrible noise it made.

"There you are," a shorter, dark haired man who sat at one of the desks said. "They just left with the prisoners." He nodded in the direction of the broken door.

"Good riddance," Jamie remarked.

Alison watched as Jamie walked right across the office, stepping over papers and other things that littered the floor. Nobody batted an eye. Aidan and that Heidi woman were sitting together at one of the other desks sorting through piles of loose paperwork, and the man who Jamie had just spoken to was already focused on his computer screen again.

"Kyle, what's the damage?" Jamie asked the man, while opening the bottom drawer of his desk and pulling out some sweat pants and a T-shirt, putting the former on first.

"Managed to retrieve the hard drive. Data's fine. Your monitor is cracked, but we've got a spare. Whatever papers they had planned to take, the Alliance guys handed 'em over to us before they took them all away."

Jamie nodded, then pulled the T-shirt over his head and returned to Alison who still stood awkwardly by the door.

"Guys, listen up," Jamie raised his voice slightly.

Aidan and Heidi looked up in his direction, as did the other guy he'd just identified as Kyle.

"What happened today was extremely unfortunate. I know you all have your own theories about how our location was compromised, but I just want to say that I take full responsibility. It was my job to keep this place safe, and I've failed you. The Alliance council will investigate, and Adrian Blacke will probably want to question every one of you individually. I can't tell you what to say, but-"

"Now hang on." Aidan got up. "They knew our faces from Heidi's rescue. They could have followed any one of us here."

"They could have, but they didn't." Jamie looked serious.

Alison's heart was hammering in her chest. Was he going to tell them everything? Could they trust these people to keep their secret? It was bad enough that Alison had lost everyone from her past, would the same happen to Jamie if his people disapproved of their relationship?

"Boss," Heidi said.

Jamie nodded at her. "Yeah?"

"I know what we said earlier, but it's obvious that Alison's help was instrumental in keeping us all safe. Aidan said as much already."

"Thanks," Alison mumbled.

"I agree. And that's what we'll tell Mr. Blacke if he asks. Unless the prisoners talk, we'll never find out how exactly they managed to track us down," the other man, Kyle, said.

"Glad to hear it. Thanks, Kyle. Heidi." Jamie nodded at all three of them, and they settled back into whatever it was they'd been doing before Jamie had interrupted them.

What the hell had just happened? That was it? That was the entire briefing? Alison couldn't believe her ears.

Not wordy enough for you? Jamie smiled at her. *They're good people. It'll be fine.*

"Okay then. Carry on while I make sure Alison gets home safely, all right? It's the least I can do after all she's done for us."

"No problem, Boss," Heidi responded. "We've got

this."

The other two men remained silent. All the while when Jamie was talking, so much was left unsaid their chat had been downright vague and confusing. Alison wished she could listen in on everyone else's heads too. Perhaps it was for the best that she couldn't, though, because finding out everyone's true feelings might just make things even weirder.

Still, Alison was kind of glad that the talk hadn't dragged out further. She needed to leave this place urgently and figure out what was next for her. For them.

Let's get the hell out of here, Alison thought.

Jamie grabbed his coat and marched straight to the door, Alison followed. She still couldn't believe that everyone had just accepted Jamie's non-explanation, after everything that had happened during the fight. Gareth had spelled out exactly what was going on between her and Jamie, and yet it hadn't made any difference?

These people were weird. Either very trusting, or very indifferent.

Outside, the weather was as nice as it had been all morning. As if nothing had happened. Clear blue skies, bright sunshine that even managed to warm Alison's back as they walked. Jamie seemed in a rush to get away from the Alliance building, as was Alison.

They walked at a brisk pace, turned a few corners away from the quiet streets of the warehouse district until finally risking a bit more affection.

"How do you know they're okay with us being together?" Alison asked. "The way you'd talked about it earlier, it seemed like we were breaking all your rules?"

"Heidi and Aidan have enough problems of their own to bother with ours. Aidan shared their secret with you during the rescue, so it's understood that I'd come to know. Kyle... I don't think he really cares, to be honest."

"What about that other guy, Blacke?" Alison asked.

"He's a problem, both for us as well as for Aidan and Heidi if he ever finds out about them. We'll cross that bridge when we get to it."

"And now?" Alison thought aloud.

"Now..." Jamie turned to her and cupped her face in his hands. "Now I take you home and we forget about all that's happened today."

"Okay," Alison whispered. "Not my place, though, I don't think I can stand going back there now, after everything..." The mere thought of it hurt and she again felt the prickle of tears in her eyes.

Her little flat was full of reminders of Gareth and her dad. Exactly the kind of things she needed some time and space from. It would take a while for her to get used to her new situation, no matter how much she believed that she'd done the right thing.

Jamie rested his arm on her shoulder and Alison felt at least some of her pain melt away under his touch.

"No problem. Stay with me." He leaned down and kissed her cheek, then the side of her neck.

His affections as well as his offer made Alison smile despite herself.

"I'd like that."

With Jamie's hand traveling up and around her neck, guiding their lips together, things didn't seem so bad anymore. For all that she'd lost, she'd gained something too. A future, with the boy she'd first met so many years ago and whom she'd never managed to completely forget.

He'd explained bears believe that fate brings couples together. It was tempting to think that everything that had happened, including his brother's abduction and her own crazy upbringing, had somehow served a greater purpose.

She would have never met him if it hadn't been for her dad and his radical affiliations.

He kissed her intensely, his hunger for her fanning her own.

Not here, she thought, and grabbed his other hand, running her fingers across his. His hand was so much bigger, stronger, and yet so very gentle and comforting as well. He managed to make her feel small, protected and safe at last.

Jamie's eyes darkened as he stared at her. His mind grew clouded with the possibilities that lay ahead once they reached his place. Glimpses of the imagery in his mind spilled over into hers: their naked bodies entwined, doing what they did best.

He didn't need further encouragement. Resolutely they started to walk again, keen to reach their destination only a few blocks away.

It didn't take them long, and they already had their hands all over each other by the time they reached the front door of his apartment. The first items of clothing ended up in the hallway, the rest were discarded by the time they'd reached the bedroom.

Jamie knelt down on the ground and forced her down onto her knees on top of the edge of the bed just in front of him. He dove into her without warning, tasting her sweet essence, covering her already wet lips with his mouth.

Alison grabbed handfuls of the pillow, moaning loudly as he explored her depths with his tongue. "Oh god, Jamie!"

He didn't pause or hesitate, instead licked her even more deeply.

Alison's legs threatened to buckle with the intensity of his affections. Out of breath and control, her mind went blank and she closed her eyes to focus on the pleasure he was intent on giving her.

I'm sorry everything happened the way it did, but I love you, she heard Jamie's voice in her mind.

She wanted to respond, to say that things would work out somehow and she loved him too, but she couldn't muster the energy. Every fiber in her body was primed, so ready to let go.

When he reached around and started to manipulate her clit, with his tongue still inside of her, it was all she could take. His hands were electric, his mouth was magical. He knew how to please her instinctively, effortlessly. She'd never had a lover like him before.

Her release sneaked up on her, making her knees shake until she sunk down into the soft mattress, shivering and moaning in between labored breaths.

I love you too, she finally responded, when she found her wits again.

He turned her over so they were facing each other and climbed on top of the bed as well. His hands cupped her face as he gazed into her eyes. His eyes were so blue, full of love and hope. In some ways he was still that wide-eyed boy from twenty years ago.

"Crazy to think we've only been together for a few days," he whispered. "I can't imagine a life without you anymore."

All the hairs on her arms stood up as he spoke.

"I know. Tell me this won't change. Tell me our feelings will never fade..." Alison demanded.

She knew what he was going to say, and that her question was unnecessary, but she couldn't get enough of his voice.

"Never. Our bond will grow every day, the longer we are together. Every day we spend together will be better than the last."

Alison closed her eyes and smiled, when his lips found hers once more.

They spent the rest of the night making love, until inevitably, the two of them fell asleep in each other's arms.

CHAPTER ELEVEN

"Morning, sleepyhead." Alison greeted Jamie with a smile on her face and steamy mug of coffee in hand.

Jamie smiled, and stretched out the lethargy from his limbs. What a night.

"You're up early," he remarked, stifling a yawn.

"Not quite. But I couldn't bear to wake you earlier, you really are too cute when you're asleep."

Jamie propped himself up on his elbows and gave her a sideways look. "If you say so. What's the time?" He leaned over and checked the alarm clock on the bedside table.

"Whoa, eight already?" Within a split second, he was up and halfway across the room, heading straight for the en-suite.

"At least have your coffee," Alison called after him.

"Okay."

He didn't have much time. Normally he'd have turned up at work by now. The others would be wondering where he was and what he was up to. It was one thing for him to be involved with a human, another to rub it in people's faces.

Jamie rushed through his morning routine and was ready in record time, though he did stop to take a big gulp from the mug Alison had poured for him. Extra sugar, just how he liked it. It was still hot, but just the right fuel to keep up his momentum.

He gave her a quick peck on the cheek, grabbed his coat and was halfway out the door when he noticed someone waiting by the front steps.

"Kyle! I was just heading out," Jamie said.

Kyle brushed away his explanation with a casual hand gesture. "We need to talk."

Shit, he wasn't about to get a lecture from a most unlikely source, was he? Jamie took a deep breath and straightened himself, well aware that with his shoulders pushed back, he towered over the man by at least a foot.

"You know that thing you asked me to look into?" Kyle asked, retrieving the brown paper dossier from his shoulder bag. The same one Jamie had given him just days ago.

"Yeah."

"I've made some progress."

Jamie allowed himself to relax a bit, though he couldn't quite read Kyle enough to figure out whether whatever he'd found out was good or bad news.

"Not here. Please come in," Jamie said.

Kyle nodded and followed him inside, waiting until the door had safely shut behind the two of them before continuing. "I've updated the file as you can see. Found a location."

He handed it to Jamie right there in the hallway.

"That's brilliant, great job!" Jamie eagerly took the file and started leafing through the new pages.

There was a map of a residential area in Glasgow with a red circle in the center, presumably the exact address, as well as pictures of the same area downloaded from Google street view.

There was also a photograph. It looked very recent. A pair of brilliant blue eyes that rivaled his own, the same shade of brown hair as Jamie remembered. It was unmistakably him.

"That's him. He goes by the name Matthew Argyle now," Kyle spoke deliberately, maintaining eye contact with Jamie throughout, which was unusual for him. "It took me a little while, putting two-and-two together. But here ya go."

Jamie looked down at the photo again. Despite the passing years there was no doubt in his mind that this was his little brother. He flipped the page over to find a print-out of an old newspaper article detailing the disappearance. The highlighted portions attracted his eye immediately.

'... Matthew (Matty) Brown, vanished from Applecross...'

'... his brother, Jamie Brown, and his parents...'

Kyle was still staring at Jamie's face when he looked up from the article.

"He's confused, as far as I can tell from his online activities. Doesn't quite understand where he belongs. It's time to bring him home," Kyle said, his tone uncharacteristically confident and sure of himself.

It was as though, just for a brief moment, Kyle was the one in charge. Jamie nodded.

"Well then, see you at the office." Kyle smiled at him briefly and opened the front door, leaving Jamie behind clutching the file.

He couldn't help himself and opened it to the photograph again. There he was. Matty. He'd been so young when he'd gone missing that one of the only things Jamie remembered about him was his obsession for sand castles. What was he like now? Would he even remember the family he'd been taken from so many years ago?

"Jamie." Alison appeared behind him, resting her hand on his back. "You've found him! Congratulations!"

Jamie turned to face her, his heart warming to the radiant smile on her face. "Don't congratulate me yet. What if he doesn't know who I am? I'd just be some stranger trying to take him from everything he knows all over again."

Alison wrapped her arms around Jamie's neck. "That's not going to happen. He'll be pleased to see you again, I can guarantee it."

Jamie felt that she really believed every word of what she was saying, but that didn't change the concerns that still weighed on him. *What if Alison's dad was right and Matty had grown up all human?*

"I'd better go now," he said, then kissed her goodbye again.

So much to do, so little time. If Jamie was going to go see Matty in Glasgow, he had to ensure everything at the office would be fine during his absence.

"He was wrong, you know," Alison called after Jamie. "My dad. I didn't think about it before, but... They took a few children like your brother, then all of a sudden they stopped. If his assumptions were correct, and they'd been able to reeducate those kids, why not keep going?"

Jamie turned back for a moment. She made an excellent point.

"Why indeed. I wish I could have asked him that."

"Yeah." Alison looked down at the floor, pressing her lips together. "Me too."

Jamie smiled at her, and caressed her cheek with the back of his index finger. "Will you be all right here while I'm at work?"

"Yeah. I'll be fine. I was thinking perhaps I'll move some of my things in if you don't mind."

"I don't mind at all. All this stuff-" Jamie gestured in the direction of the living room. "I don't care for it. None of it means anything. Would be nice to have something a bit more personal in here."

"Great." Alison smiled at him. "See you in the evening then."

"I can't wait." With that, Jamie turned the handle and

stepped out, ready to tackle whatever would land on his plate today. Although a part of him didn't want to leave her alone, he knew that the time spent apart would make their reunion at night all the sweeter.

Funny, how just a week ago he would have been in a rush to leave in the morning, and would aim to delay his homecoming as much as he possibly could at night. He'd been drifting, waiting endlessly for something to change.

He'd been alone, suffering the loss of his brother as well as the girl who had turned his world upside down so long ago. Now his wounds were well on their way to being mended.

His subconscious had been right: *find the girl, and he'd be whole again.* He'd found the girl, and before long he'd be reunited with Matty, too.

***

ABOUT THE AUTHOR

Dear Reader,

Thanks for reading Scottish Werebear: A Forbidden Love, Book 3 in the Scottish Werebears Series. Although this is my first published paranormal romance series, I'm not new to writing in general. In fact, my mom still tells me to this day about how I would make up stories, and attempt to record them in my clumsy, shaky handwriting from the moment I learned to read and write. From there I went on to write fan fiction and other stuff meant for my own eyes only.

I've always enjoyed stories of the paranormal. Vampires, shape shifters, witches and magic, all featured in the books I loved the most, even when I was still growing up. But it wasn't until much later that I got into romance. One of the first writers (a self-published author just like me!) I came across was Tina Folsom, via her Scanguards Vampire series. I was hooked. From there I went on to read more paranormal romance until I found a new favorite kind of hero: bear shifters, like the kind written by Milly Taiden, Zoe Chant, and T.S. Joyce. What I love about bears is how they can be all strong and independent, a bit reclusive, and almost grumpy, but they always end up having a heart of gold (plus they tend to know their food, and we all know that a man who can cook is doubly sexy). All that (except for the shifting into a powerful bear) almost exactly describes the sort of man I ended up falling for and marrying in real life, so it's no surprise that this is what I started my publishing career with.

To find out more, check:
LoreleiMoone.com (And why not sign up for the newsletter to be the first to find out about new releases.)

You can also get in touch with me via Facebook (search for Lorelei Moone), or email at info@loreleimoone.com

I also write contemporary romance as L. Moone. If that's something you're interested in, you can take a look at LMoone.com.

x Lorelei

www.ingramcontent.com/pod-product-compliance
Lightning Source LLC
Chambersburg PA
CBHW070450170726
48291CB00005B/1693